She glanced up, caught by his lingering gaze.

A breeze lifted her hair off her shoulders and she shivered, more from Adam's closeness than the cool air.

Adam shrugged out of the light denim jacket he'd worn outside. Reaching behind her, he wrapped it around her shoulders, then pulled her even closer.

She went willingly. Into his arms. His warmth. There was no future for them. She planned to leave Resolute for someplace with more opportunities, where she could earn decent money and provide a better life for her kids.

But she *wanted* to kiss him. She had for more than a decade. She'd dreamed about what might have been if he'd asked her out when they were teenagers. When life had stretched before them with endless opportunities. Only, he hadn't. And she'd stopped waiting for him, saving her dreams for her fantasies.

RESOLUTE INVESTIGATION

LESLIE MARSHMAN

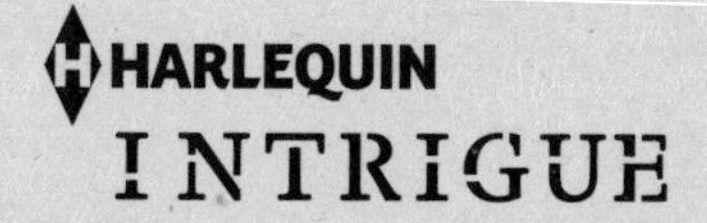

To Cori

Thank you for loving my books from the very beginning. You've advised me, cheered me on, celebrated my publishing highs and lifted me from the depths of deadline hells. You've helped to make every book I write better, and there's no one I'd rather have by my side on this wild journey. I'm forever grateful.

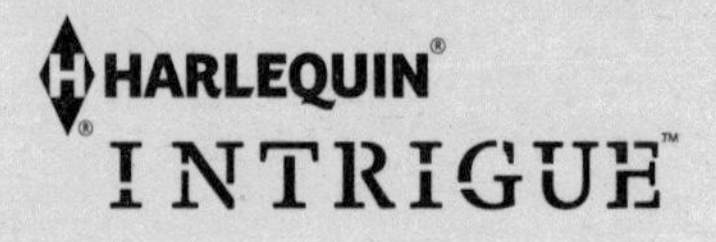

Recycling programs for this product may not exist in your area.

ISBN-13: 978-1-335-59119-7

Resolute Investigation

For questions and comments about the quality of this book, please contact us at CustomerService@Harlequin.com.

Harlequin Enterprises ULC
22 Adelaide St. West, 41st Floor
Toronto, Ontario M5H 4E3, Canada
www.Harlequin.com

Printed in U.S.A.

Multi-award-winning author **Leslie Marshman** writes novels featuring strong heroines, the heroes who love them and the bad guys who fear them. She called Denver home until she married a Texan without reading the fine print. Now she lives halfway between Houston and Galveston and embraces the humidity. When Leslie's not writing, you might find her camping at a lake, fishing pole in one hand and a book in the other. Visit her at www.lesliemarshman.com, www.Facebook.com/lesliemarshmanauthor, www.Instagram.com/leslie_marshman or @lesliemarshman on Twitter.

Books by Leslie Marshman

Harlequin Intrigue

The Protectors of Boone County, Texas

Resolute Justice
Resolute Aim
Resolute Investigation

Scent Detection

Visit the Author Profile page at Harlequin.com.

CAST OF CHARACTERS

Adam Reed—Chief deputy to Boone County sheriff Cassie Reed, he's the second oldest of the four Reed siblings. With his sister off on her honeymoon, Adam's in charge of the Sheriff's Department and determined to keep Resolute safe. But can he remain impartial when tragedy strikes close to home?

Rachel Miller—The waitress at the Busy B Café has her hands full between work, online college classes and raising two small children on her own. Adam had a crush on her in high school that's never gone away. But Rachel has plans that are bigger than Resolute.

Eric Miller—Rachel's ex-husband. She kicked him to the curb the day she caught him cheating when she was pregnant. And even now her life would be much easier without him in it.

Noah Reed—One of Adam's younger twin brothers, also a deputy. He's taking on more responsibilities at work and settling down with his fiancée, Bree Delgado. But nothing can diminish his offbeat sense of humor.

Bree Delgado—A former San Antonio cop, Bree's now a Boone County deputy. Her quick eye for detail makes her an investigative powerhouse within the department. Since moving to Resolute, she's become good friends with Rachel.

Chapter One

Chief Deputy Adam Reed snaked his way through the Friday-night crowd of spectators, a tired-looking horde reeking of booze, sweat and desperation. It was two in the morning, closing time. Bad luck for him to be on call but here he was, breaking up a fight that had begun inside the Dead End bar, then spilled through the doors and into the parking lot.

Max, both bartender and owner, had called it in to the Boone County Sheriff's Department, claiming Eric Miller had started the whole thing. Max wanted him arrested for damages to the establishment. Adam scoffed. The Dead End was no more an establishment than the dumpster out back was a receptacle. The place was a dive bar, plain and simple.

Some in the mob shoved back as Adam elbowed through, but when they noticed who they were pushing, even the drunken patrons apologized and shuffled sideways. Breaking through the innermost ring of bystanders, he stopped and took in the view. A light spring rain had ended minutes earlier, and the bar's neon sign reflected off the wet asphalt. Eric, his face bloodied and already swelling, faced off against a shorter but powerfully built man Adam hadn't seen before. They circled each other, throwing jabs and punches.

"Enough. Step away from each other." Adam issued the order in an authoritative voice and gave the two combatants a moment to follow his demand. Not likely to happen, but always worth a try.

Both men glanced at him, then apparently decided to finish their fight before the law could intervene. At least, the stranger did. He curled his left hand into a fist and swung before Adam could act. Eric took a brutal uppercut to his chin. His head jerked back violently, and he staggered. Shaking away the stars he must have been seeing, his eyes narrowed. Then, like a bull enraged by the matador's blood-red muleta, Eric charged, fists swinging, pummeling the other man with ineffectual blows.

Adam grabbed Eric's shirt collar and pulled him back several paces, then turned toward the stranger. Just in time to be blindsided by the full force of a roundhouse punch to the side of his head.

He hadn't seen that one coming, literally or figuratively.

His ears ringing and his vision blurred, Adam staggered sideways and went down on one knee. Two men in the crowd looped their arms beneath Adam's, keeping him from going horizontal on the wet pavement.

An agitated female voice called out, "Someone call 9-1-1."

Adam made it back to a standing position with help from the men.

"Lady, I *am* 9-1-1." He got his bearings and shook his head, everything falling back into place.

He blinked a few times, then peered toward the two fighters, worried he might see four of them. But as his vision cleared, only one, Eric Miller, stood in front of him.

"Where's the other guy?" Adam asked, surveying the crowd.

Still drunk, Eric swayed on his feet. "He disappeared right after he clocked you."

"Who was he?" Adam pulled his cuffs from his duty belt. "The guy you were fighting?"

"No idea."

Adam gave him a skeptical look and motioned for him to hold out his arms. "Eric Miller, you're under arrest for drunk and disorderly conduct and destruction of property. You have the right to remain silent…" Adam went through the spiel while cuffing him with his arms in front. Eric was done fighting for the night.

"What were you fighting about, anyway?"

Eric shrugged.

"Well, you'll have plenty of time to remember while you sober up in a cell."

"Come on, Adam. The other guy started it. I was just defending myself." He perked up a little. "I told Rach I'd watch the kids tomorrow. You wouldn't want me to disappoint them, right?"

"Yeah, right. You don't care about your kids any more than you ever cared about Rachel." Adam had overheard enough snippets of conversation between Rachel and her boss, Marge, to figure that out.

Adam walked the cuffed man to his cruiser and loaded him in the back seat, then glanced at his watch. Almost two thirty. Eric wouldn't be arraigned until Monday. That gave Adam two days to question Eric and get the name of the stranger who'd sucker punched him.

There was something about the stranger that piqued his curiosity. He couldn't quite put his finger on why, but he was sure Eric knew the man.

Driving to the justice center, he glanced in his rearview mirror at Eric, already passed out and drooling. Adam would never understand how any man married to Rachel could be dumb enough to let her go. Dumb enough to choose booze and adultery over the incredible woman he had at home.

At least Rachel had the sense to divorce the bum as soon as she found out about his cheating.

Adam had had a crush on Rachel Novotny since the day she'd beat him in their middle school's pitch, hit and run competition. She'd never paid him any attention, and he'd been too shy to start a conversation with her. Each school year he'd promised himself that he would talk to her. Get to know her. Ask her out. And each year he'd chickened out.

Realistically, what could he have offered her back then? She was smart, athletic and beautiful. And he was just…what? Smart, but not as smart as her. She'd started school early, so even though she was two years younger than him, she was only one grade behind. He'd held his own in sports, but Nate was always the athletic brother in their family. And while he was no slouch in the looks department, she'd been…a goddess. Still was.

Her thick blond hair had always been long and wavy. He wanted to drag his fingers through its smoothness, its silkiness. And her eyes—oh, those bewitching eyes! They alternated between pale green and blue depending on what she wore or even her mood. It was almost a game for him to guess their color before he saw them.

He'd had one serious relationship in college. At least, he'd *thought* it was serious. But when the woman had pressured him for a long-term commitment, he couldn't make one. It was Rachel he wanted. By the time he'd returned to Resolute with a BS in criminal justice from Sam Houston State, Rachel was married to Eric and working at the Busy B Café.

A bitter pill to swallow, but he'd learned from it. Once his heart had healed, Adam built a stone fortress around it for protection. Imaginary, but it did the job.

Since her divorce, Rachel's job at the diner and his frequent patronage there offered him plenty of opportunities. They spoke, joked, smiled at each other.

But still the fortress held.

When Adam bumped over a set of railroad tracks, Eric's head lolled back against the seat, and he started mumbling.

"Can't understand you, Miller. What are you talking about?" Adam checked the mirror, made sure his passenger wasn't choking. He wasn't. "You talking about your friend at the bar? Your boxing buddy?"

More incoherent mumbling.

"What the heck did you do to that guy to get him that ticked off at you?" Adam asked, talking to himself more than to Miller.

As his head rolled toward his chest again, Miller uttered one clear word. "Dead."

Interesting. Didn't mean anything, but still, an interesting word to blurt out.

"You feeling so bad, you wish you were dead? You're mad at me and wish I was dead?" He couldn't believe he was having this one-sided conversation, but at least it passed the time. "Who's dead, Eric? Your buddy at the bar?"

He took a left turn into the center's back parking lot, the access to the jail entrance. Eric jostled with the turn, and Adam's gaze flicked to the mirror and held there.

As if possessed, Eric sat upright, his blank eyes wide with what looked like terror. "He was dead, but now he's back for me," he said in a calm, clear voice.

Then he slumped, leaned forward and threw up all over Adam's cruiser.

THE BUSY B's Monday lunch crowd seemed larger than usual. And louder. Picking up a tray of dirty dishes, Rachel speed-walked from table eight to the kitchen, wishing she'd taken something earlier for her stress headache. Anger had brought on the pounding inside of her skull, the pain beating a relentless rhythm behind her eyes ever since Saturday morning when Eric hadn't shown up to take the kids.

Surprise, surprise.

A man held up his mug. "Darlin', can I get more coffee?"

"Be right there, Harold." Rachel took an order from

another booth, sped to the kitchen pass-through and stuck it in the ticket carousel, grabbed one carafe of regular and one of decaf, and filled Harold's mug before he asked again. She made a route through the diner, topping off every mug, her anger still simmering.

With her mom visiting a friend in San Antonio and an important project due for one of her online college courses, she'd asked Marge for the weekend off and asked Eric to switch weekends with her. He'd managed to dry out and shape up enough before the custody hearing to get the kids every other weekend—though, it still shocked her that he wanted them at all.

Even so, she'd managed to work out an amicable schedule that was flexible for them both when necessary. And this past weekend had been necessary.

She'd worked on the project as much as possible while caring for Brad, almost five, and ten-month-old Daisy. Which wasn't very much.

Then, to top it off, her deadbeat ex-husband woke her up early this morning and asked her to bail him out of jail. *Jail!*

He actually had the nerve to get mad at *her* when she refused. For all she cared, his sorry butt could rot in a cell. Be easier to find him when it came time to serve him for zero child-support payments.

"Rachel." Marge, owner of the Busy B, called her name.

She glanced toward her boss and groaned.

Speak of the devil.

Marge's ample frame was blocking Eric from getting past the front counter. Her face burning with unspent rage, Rachel strode through the diner and stopped behind Marge.

She took in Eric's bruised and battered face, pleased that she held not one speck of sympathy or compassion for him. "What do you want?"

"I need to talk to you." His eyes darted around the diner and desperation filled his voice.

"I'm working." She tried to keep her expression neutral, what with the place filled to capacity and most of the customers watching the exchange. "Go away," she managed between clenched teeth.

"It'll only take a minute. But it can't wait." He fidgeted. "Please."

Rachel glanced at Marge.

Sighing, as if disappointed with Rachel for the unasked question, Marge stepped aside. "If you want to talk to him, go ahead. Best to do it outside." Marge glared at Eric, then met Rachel's eyes. "And if you don't want to talk to him, I'll have Adam remove him from the premises."

Damn. She'd forgotten Adam was here. Rachel died a little on the inside knowing he was a witness to her humiliation. A member of the prestigious Reed family, he no doubt disapproved of very public displays of domestic problems.

Eric's intake of breath was loud as he looked over Rachel's shoulder at the chief deputy.

She pictured Adam's broad, square shoulders and straight spine, sitting in a nearby booth within earshot. She hoped her loser ex was properly intimidated by the gun-toting lawman.

"Just one minute, Rach. I swear."

"Fine. Outside. And don't call me Rach." She followed him out the door, partway down the sidewalk, and checked her watch. "Your minute starts now."

"Look, I'm sorry I couldn't watch the kids this weekend." His phony tone of apology was one she'd heard often before.

"You've got the *sorry* part right." Her fury reached the surface. "You promised you'd take Brad and Daisy. Brad was in tears when you didn't show. And you knew how important that project was for my class. Thanks to you, I'll have to turn it in late." Her hands curled up and released in a continuous pattern. "And your excuse is that you got yourself arrested?"

"It wasn't my fault. Some guy started a fight with me." He shrugged.

Rachel couldn't help the snort that escaped. "It's never your fault, is it? Out getting drunk at the Dead End, I suppose." It never failed to amaze her how often he could use the same excuse and expect it to work. "And if it wasn't your fault, why were you arrested?"

"The other guy ran. He punched Adam and disappeared." His eyes narrowed. "By the way, thanks for bailing me out."

Shaking her head, Rachel's lips curled in disgust. Disgust that she'd ever loved this man. "And why would I? You've never given me a single dime toward child support, and you expect me to save you every time you screw up." She scoffed. "Maybe you should have called your latest *girlfriend*." She couldn't stop herself from using air quotes.

Eric threw his hands up in the air. "Whatever. Where are Brad's backpack and Daisy's diaper bag?"

Definitely not the important topic she'd expected. "I had so much extra time this morning after you woke me, I went by your apartment and picked them up."

"I need them back. And my spare key while you're at it." When she hesitated, he grabbed her upper arm and squeezed it. "It's a matter of life and death."

Rachel yanked her arm from his grasp. "Don't sound so dramatic." Mimicking him in a sarcastic voice, she said, "Ooh, I'll just die if I don't get to see my kids." She rolled her eyes. "You don't need the bags back. You're done getting the kids."

"We've got a custody agreement. There's nothing you can do about it."

Rachel leaned toward him. "Wanna bet? I'll haul you back into court, and when the judge hears you're still getting drunk and fighting—not to mention arrested—and you still haven't started paying support, he'll award me full custody."

"You're insane. You'll never win in court." This time, Eric laughed. "Who would award full custody to an uneducated diner waitress who lives in her mother's garage?"

"Better than a no-account drunk who spends his under-the-table cash wages—when he can manage to keep a job long enough to get them—on loose women and booze instead of diapers and groceries for his kids."

All amusement gone from his voice, Eric took a step toward her, making Rachel step back. "Just try and take my kids, Rach. See how that works out for you." His voice, low and menacing, sent a chill racing down her spine.

Tears threatened. From frustration, from fear, from lost love and newfound regret and despair that not only was this her life but also it would always be her life with this man as her children's father. Unless she did something about it.

Stepping back into his space, Rachel's voice rose like the tide of emotions welling up inside her. "You'll never spend another minute with *my* children." Pointing her index finger, she jabbed at his chest to accentuate her words, taking great pleasure when he winced and stepped away from her. "And if you try to, so help me God, I'll make sure it's the last thing you ever do."

As she spun around to go back in the diner, she noticed people on the street staring at her. Every passerby had stopped to take in the show. *Nothing like airing dirty laundry in public.*

She glanced toward the diner, and her heart sank. Everyone inside was staring through the windows at her, getting a front-row view of that dirty laundry.

Including Adam Reed.

Chapter Two

Friday morning, Adam stopped at Helen Gibson's desk on his way in and handed her a small bag. The department's administrative assistant and dispatcher loved a good prune Danish.

"Thank you, sweetie." Helen peeked inside the bag. "With Sheriff Cassie away on her honeymoon, figured I'd be doing without my usual end-of-week treat." She reached into the bag and pulled out the pastry, which she set on a napkin with care. Mess was not tolerated in Helen's world. "You always were my favorite, you know."

"I bet you say that to all the Reeds."

"You're right, I do." Helen took a small bite. "But I only mean it when I say it to you."

"And you tell all the Reeds *that*, too." He chuckled. "By the way, when did you start calling my sister Sheriff Cassie?"

"You mean instead of what I call her when she's talking back to me? Or instead of Sheriff Reed, which was a perfectly respectable way to address her until she went and got married. Sheriff Cassie Reed-Bishop—" she wrinkled her nose "—what a mouthful."

The petite older woman had worked for the sheriff's department the entire time his father, Wallace Reed, had been sheriff. When Adam's mother had abandoned the family, Cassie had taken on the job of raising her three younger brothers, despite being just eleven herself. To help her carry the weight, Helen had answered Cassie's questions, given her a shoulder to cry on and acted as a surrogate mom to all of them.

The phone rang, and Helen grabbed the receiver. "Boone County Sheriff's Office."

She began typing information from the caller into her computer, her smile disappearing. After hanging up, she looked at Adam.

"A woman in the Oak View Apartments says there's a terrible stench coming from the unit next to hers. Says it's been getting worse each day."

"I'll take it. Send me the apartment number and caller's info." Adam headed back out the front door of the Boone County Justice Center, his breakfast sandwich he'd enjoyed minutes earlier now forming a lump in his stomach.

The only apartment complex in town, Oak View's residents were mainly people living paycheck to paycheck or old folks whose next destination would be either a nursing home or the morgue. Calls like this usually meant that for one of the older residents, Oak View had become their final resting place.

Adam hated starting the day with a cadaver.

Ten minutes later, he parked in Oak View's lot and

tracked down Ron, who'd managed the complex for decades.

"Number 312, huh?" The tall, lanky man sorted through his key ring as they rode up in the elevator. "That's Eric Miller's apartment."

Eric Miller? First the bar fight, then a public argument with Rachel, and now a rank smell coming from his place. Adam went on high alert.

"Whoo-golly." Ron waved a hand in front of his nose as they approached the third-floor apartment. "That's one rank odor."

An odor Adam had encountered before in his line of work.

"Give me the key and step back." No telling what, or who, he'd find, and he wanted the manager a safe distance away. "How many rooms inside?"

Ron didn't have to be told twice. Scooting down the hall, he said, "Just one bed, one bath. Living area and kitchen."

After drawing his Glock 22, Adam inserted the key and unlocked the apartment. When he pushed it, the door swung in, and death's putrid fragrance wafted out. The manager gagged and backed farther down the hall.

"Sheriff's Department," Adam called out, giving his eyes a moment to adjust to the dim interior before stepping over the threshold.

The tiny kitchen to his right was messy, but otherwise empty. Moving into the living area, he found the source of the stench. A body lay on the floor in a pool of dried blood.

Adam moved on to secure the rest of the apartment.

Down a short hall to the left, he cleared the bedroom and bath. Eric's housekeeping seemed lacking, but it was obvious someone had ransacked the place. Dresser drawers were dumped on the floor, the closet had been tossed, mattress and pillows slashed open.

After holstering his gun, he took out a pair of nitrile gloves from his pocket and donned them, then returned to the living area. He flipped on the overhead light, and the scene lit up in all its gruesome glory.

Pulling out his phone to take pictures, Adam crouched next to the body, ignoring droning flies and looking past maggots in the man's eyes and wounds. He'd have a better idea after the autopsy, but between the insect activity and skin discoloration, this had happened earlier in the week. Six—no, seven—stab wounds to the chest. A brutal death. Personal. One filled with fury.

If he were to guess, the high, long slash was the death blow. It appeared the weapon had hit the clavicle, slid up at an angle and sliced the carotid artery, causing a rapid bleed-out. Arterial spray and the amount of blood pooled next to the upper left side of the body supported that.

Definitely not a natural death.

But definitely Eric Miller.

Adam stood and surveyed the room. Like the bedroom, the living area had been pillaged. Couch cushions slashed, chairs overturned, anything breakable now on the floor in pieces. Then his gaze landed on a disturbing sight he'd been trying to ignore.

Lying near Eric, covered in blood, was a teddy bear.

Fear, hot and stinging, coursed through Adam's gut.

The kids. Were they here when this happened? Had they been taken?

And Rachel? Adam hadn't seen her since her fight with Eric several days ago. Had *she* been here? As another victim, or…?

Sickened by the direction of his thoughts, Adam fought against a band tightening around his chest, squeezing until he couldn't breathe.

He had to find Rachel and the kids, and he had to find them alive and well. And innocent.

"I ALREADY CALLED for the crime-scene team from Austin and the justice of the peace." Adam stood in the hallway just outside Eric's closed door, talking to Helen. "But send Noah here to keep the scene secure."

"Will do. And where will you be?" Helen liked to keep track of all the deputies. For incoming service calls, but also for their own safety.

"I need to find Rachel. Make sure she and the kids are okay."

"Is there any reason to think they're not?" The concern in her voice came through clear as a bell.

"I just want to make sure. I tried her several times between the other calls, but I kept getting her voice mail." He inhaled, death's lingering scent still clinging to the inside of his nose. "I'll need to notify her of Eric's death anyway."

"I'll get everyone moving. Noah's already on his way, shouldn't be more than five minutes." Helen paused. "Adam, I know how you've felt about Rachel since you were a kid, and I can't imagine her hurting a fly. So don't take this the wrong way, but you know as well as I do that family is always on the suspect list. That, taken together with the big fight she had with Eric the other day in front of darn near everyone in town, only makes her more of a suspect. Just my way of reminding you to stay objective."

He bit off a sharp *Always* before stabbing the red End Call button.

Fuming about Helen's implications, he paced the hallway while waiting for Noah to arrive. The very idea that Rachel had killed Eric was ridiculous. Laughable, even. He may not have exchanged much more than pleasantries with her over the past several years, but he was well aware of the kind of person she was. On the inside. Where it mattered. She simply wasn't capable of that kind of violence. Helen's not-so-subtle hint that he might not handle the investigation like any other—following the clues no matter where they led—rankled.

Then, the irony hit him. In his mind—no, in his heart—Adam had already decided Rachel hadn't done it. But statistics didn't support his belief. Neither did the evidence, circumstantial though it was. Whatever he thought about her personally, Rachel was a suspect. The prime suspect at this point, and he needed to remember that.

Thanks, Helen. He dragged his fingers through his hair, frustrated with the realization that he'd need to set his feelings for Rachel aside and remain impartial.

Still, for his peace of mind, Adam dialed the Busy B. If she was working the morning shift, he could swing by the diner and pick her up. With his office only a few blocks away, he could conduct an official interview and have her back at work within an hour. *Hopefully.*

Lee Hayes, the new short-order cook, answered.

"Is Rachel there?"

"Nope. She's off for a couple of days. You can probably catch her at home."

"Thanks." He ended the call.

When Noah arrived, Adam showed him the crime scene, then moved them back to the hallway and closed the door again. "I just need you to wait out here in the hall for the forensics investigators and the JP. I'm going to go talk to Rachel."

Noah's brows rose. "Talk to her, or question her?"

"You're not going to start on that, too, are you?"

"Ah. So, Helen's already lectured you, has she?"

"She has, and I don't need another one from you."

Lifting his hands in a defensive stance, Noah kept his tone neutral. "Hey, bro, I'm only saying that I get this might be tough for you. Treat her as a suspect, and you risk alienating her. But if you don't, you won't be your usual kick-butt-and-take-names self." He shrugged. "Maybe you should consider letting Pete or Sean take over this case."

Both Pete Grant and Sean Cavanaugh, senior deputies, were good. But this case was his. "Come on, Noah. You know department protocol as well as I do. Either Cassie or I take lead on murders. With her gone, it falls to me. And I'm perfectly capable of doing my job without being biased toward Rachel." He fought a growing kernel of self-righteousness. Everything Noah said was true, but his baby brother didn't have to know that. Without another word, Adam walked away, resolved to make his boast true.

He headed for Rachel's mother's house. The Novotnys had built a mother-in-law apartment above their detached garage when Rachel had been in middle school. Neither mother-in-law had accepted their gracious offer, so Rachel and Eric had moved into it when they'd married. Rachel and her kids still lived there, with her mom watching the little ones while Rachel worked.

Adam drove up the long driveway to the garage, which sat far enough behind and to the side of the main house to enjoy its own privacy. He noticed Rachel before he even stepped out of his cruiser.

Wearing shorts and a V-neck T-shirt, she knelt in front of a landscaped area of flowers, digging with a trowel. Her long hair was pulled up in a casual ponytail on top of her head, loose tendrils falling around her face. She'd gotten to her feet when he pulled in and parked, and she kept her eyes on him as he walked toward her. Taking off her left gardening glove, she brushed away the stray tendrils with the back of her hand and smiled.

"Hi, Adam. What brings you out here?"

Her face, glistening with perspiration, stole his breath. Her damp shirt, clinging to her body, shut down his mind. When she tipped her head to the side and stared at him as if he'd lost the ability to speak, he forced every part of his body back to professional mode.

"Just wanted to make sure you and the kids were okay."

Her brows pinched into a frown. "Of course we are. Why wouldn't we be?" She squinted at him, one hand acting as a visor against the sun. "If you're talking about that argument Eric and I had the other day, it was nothing. Just him being his usual self and me reacting to it."

Adam nodded. "Where are the kids?"

"Inside with Mom. I needed some alone time, and gardening always relaxes me." She glanced down at the seedlings waiting to go into the ground. "I've always loved plants more than cut flowers. Bouquets wither and die. But a potted plant with blooms will last for however long you care for it." She pulled off her right glove and slapped it against the left, knocking off loose soil. "How are *you* doing?"

"Fine, thanks..." Adam's eyes went straight to the bandage on the outside edge of her right hand.

"What happened to your hand?" His concern was real, but with her ex-husband lying dead on his apartment floor, the ulterior motive he had for asking made him feel less than honest.

Rachel twisted her wrist and inspected the bandage. "This?" She chuckled. "I was chopping vegetables for dinner night before last, and that rascal Brad sneaked up behind me and scared the living daylights out of me. I screamed, which scared him, and when he saw the blood, he started crying harder than I was from the pain." She shook her head. "Poor little guy."

Do I believe her? Or could she have cut her hand shoving a knife into her ex?

Adam studied her closely, looking for any tells that

would clue him in that she was lying. A necessity, but he still hated himself for doing it. "Is that why you're off work?"

She nodded. "As it turns out, the cut was pretty deep. I ended up getting a few stitches, and I can't carry anything in this hand. Marge told me to take a couple of days off, let it heal."

"Rachel…uh, there's no easy way to say this." Adam waited until she met his eyes with a questioning look. "I'm here to inform you that Eric is dead."

Rachel's mouth fell open. "What?"

"His body was found this morning." Adam didn't add that he was the one who had found him.

Her face scrunched in disbelief. "I don't understand. He can't be dead. I just saw him on Monday, and it's not like he has a fatal disease." Shaking her head as if to dislodge the words, she asked, "Are you sure?"

Adam nodded. "I came by because I wanted to let you know before you heard it anywhere else."

"Thanks, I guess. This must be one of your least favorite tasks."

So like Rachel, to think of others even at a time like this. No way a woman with such a big heart could have plunged a sharp object into someone else's. "Part of the job."

"How did it happen? A car accident?" Her eyes narrowed in anger. "Was he drunk? Did he hurt anyone else? I kept telling him—"

"Rachel, Eric didn't die in an accident." He held her gaze. "I can't discuss the particulars, but right now his death is considered a homicide."

"Homicide? As in, he was mur..." Her face paled, and she took a half step to the side.

Reaching out to steady her by the elbow, he answered her unfinished question. "Yes."

Her breathing became slow and deep. "Oh Lord. How on earth am I going to explain to a five-year-old that his daddy was...murdered?" Then her eyes widened in realization. "You asked how we were when you first got here. You think the kids and I are in danger?"

"No." The thought of them being in future danger had never even occurred to him. "I was concerned that Brad and Daisy might have been at his apartment when it happened, despite the argument you two had on Monday. But they weren't, and you're all here and safe."

Her face blanched again, and he mentally kicked himself.

"Sorry, I shouldn't have mentioned that. I didn't mean to upset you." He cleared his throat. "You might want to hold off on telling the kids anything for now. Wait until we know more." Adam ached for her. And for her kids, especially her son. "You still have my cell number?" He'd made sure she and Marge kept it in their phones for the occasional problem customer at the diner.

Rachel checked her phone and confirmed she had it. Dealing with banalities seemed to calm her.

Adam wished *he* could help calm her. Give her a hug, tell her everything would be okay. But things might not be okay. And they didn't share that kind of closeness. "If you need any help explaining things to Brad, give me a call. Getting the twins to understand about our mom disappearing wasn't easy, either, and they were only a few years older than him."

"Thanks. I appreciate the offer." She looked around as if she didn't know what to do next.

He rubbed the back of his neck. "I, uh, I'll need you to come down to the justice center and answer some routine questions." Despite wanting Rachel to be innocent, the fight outside the diner, the bandaged cut on her hand, the fact that her life would be ten times easier without Eric in it niggled at him. "It's just standard operating procedure. Whenever someone is killed, the family is always interviewed."

She studied his face with an intensity that unnerved him. "Oh, I get it now. You didn't come by to make sure the kids and I were safe. You came by because you think *I* killed Eric, don't you? You think I'm a murderer."

Chapter Three

Rachel paused halfway up the steps to the justice center. Was she doing the right thing, coming here without a lawyer? Eric dead, her being questioned, it all seemed so surreal.

But she wasn't guilty. She had nothing to hide, and the sooner she answered his questions, the sooner Adam could get busy finding the real killer.

She continued up the steps, reminding herself of what Adam had said. At the beginning of a murder investigation, they always talked to family members. Especially the spouse. Especially after a divorce. Especially after a big fight, when the ex-wife might have sort of threatened the now deceased in public.

A lot of people had seen and heard that argument. *What if they think I did it?* Again, she weighed the foolishness of not retaining a lawyer. Not that she could afford one. Then, clinging to her innocence as her shield, she convinced herself she'd be fine. What the townspeople thought about her was irrelevant. She'd be leaving Resolute before summer ended.

Almost to the top landing, Rachel stopped dead in

her tracks. *What if, deep down,* Adam *thinks I did it?* Of course, he'd denied it when she flat out asked him earlier, when he came by the house to tell her about Eric. *And to gauge my reaction because he already considered me a suspect.* She covered her mouth with her hand as a broken sob escaped.

What a mess her life had become, just when she was finally getting things together.

Adam was doing his job, searching for evidence to arrest someone for this terrible crime. She'd always respected his diligence as a deputy. Appreciated his strong work ethic. That this man she so admired might think her capable of murder was far more heartbreaking to her than Eric's death.

There'd be no evidence of her involvement, which he'd learn soon enough. Because, of course, she didn't do it. She straightened her spine and continued to the door. Anyone who truly knew her would believe in her innocence. That's all there was to it.

Might as well get this over with.

As she crossed the lobby, Helen greeted her with a sympathetic smile and sad eyes. "How're you holding up, Rachel?"

"Shocked, I guess. I never imagined anyone would actually kill Eric."

"I'm sure it gave you quite the jolt." Helen straightened a stack of files on her desk that was already straight. "What can I do for you?"

"Adam asked me to come in and answer some questions." Rachel had taken her hair out of the ponytail, and now she ran her fingers through the waves hanging in front of her shoulders. The smooth, repetitive movement soothed her.

"He just left on a call." Helen picked up her phone's receiver. "Let me see if I can catch him, have him come back."

"That's okay. I can wait if you don't think he'll be gone too long." It seemed the better option than leaving and listening to the voices in her head argue for another day.

"I doubt he'll be gone long at all." Helen stood and headed for the door behind her, where Rachel guessed all the crime-solving happened. "I'm getting a bottle of water. Would you like one?"

Realizing her throat was dry, Rachel nodded. "Yes, please."

Before Helen returned with the water, Deputy Dave Sanders entered through the front door. Familiar with his unpleasant demeanor from his thankfully infrequent visits to the diner, Rachel suddenly found a need to search her messy purse for something.

"Rachel Miller, right?" He pointed at her, as if he wasn't sure.

She glanced up and nodded.

"You're here for questioning regarding the murder of your ex-husband?" Without waiting for a response, he flicked his hand in a rude *follow me* gesture and walked to the door Helen had disappeared behind. "Come on. I'll get you settled in an interrogation room."

Interrogation room? Two words, and just that fast, doubt and fear reasserted themselves in her mind. Ignoring the voice telling her to run, she stood. And despite her distaste for Deputy Sanders, Rachel's ingrained respect for law enforcement won out, and she trailed behind him to a small room with a small table and two small, uncomfortable-looking chairs.

She took a seat, expecting to wait for Adam.

Instead, Dave closed the door with an ominous finality and assumed a belligerent pose as he sat on the chair opposite her. "So. You two had quite the argument on Monday. I know. I was there when you and the victim were screaming at each other."

"We weren't screaming." In a calm and deliberate motion, Rachel sat forward on the edge of her chair and rested her forearms on the table, hands folded. "Remind me, Deputy. Where *exactly* were you when I exchanged a few heated words with my ex-husband?" He hadn't been inside the Busy B. She would have noticed.

"Close enough to hear you threaten his life. And then days later, he winds up murdered." He hooked his hands together behind his neck and stretched out his legs, looking relaxed. "Quite the coinkydink, wouldn't you say?"

"Coinkydink?" Though it wouldn't help her situation, Rachel couldn't help but smirk at the cartoonish deputy sitting across from her. "Please tell me this conversation is being recorded. I'm sure Adam and the sheriff would love to hear this part."

He sat up, suddenly all starch and vinegar. "You know what I mean. Answer the question."

Rachel narrowed her eyes. Her respect for law enforcement stopped short of this man. "No. You answer *my* question. Where exactly were you standing that you thought you heard me threaten my ex-husband?" After her argument with Eric, she'd gazed around in horror at the bystanders enthralled by her public humiliation. Dave Sanders hadn't been among them.

"Ms. Miller." His condescending drawl fired her anger. "Where I was standing is immaterial. We've already interviewed a lot of witnesses who saw your fight that day and heard you threaten him. And every single one of them will testify to that in a court of law." He nodded toward her hand. "What's up with the bandage?"

"I cut my hand chopping vegetables."

"Stitches?"

"Yes."

"So let me get this straight. You're saying you managed to have a kitchen-knife accident requiring stitches?" He leaned forward. "At the same time your ex was stabbed to death?"

Overcome with light-headedness, Rachel slowed her breathing. "Eric was *stabbed* to death?" Her dry throat ached. "Who would do something like that?"

"How 'bout we start with the obvious?" He held his hands out toward her.

"I would *never* do anything like that, even to someone I loathe." She doubted he caught the barb directed toward him. "And I don't think you have the right to—"

"Lady, in this room, I've got all the right in the world." Then his voice lowered in a way that made her skin crawl. "It'll go easier for you if you just admit it. Why not start by telling me where the murder weapon is?"

"I didn't kill him!" Her voice rose with each word. "How many times do I have to tell you that?"

"Whoa." Dave's grin became predatory. "Looks to me like you've got a problem with anger."

"I do not have a problem with anger!" Rachel shouted, instantly realizing her mistake when the expression on Dave's insincere face softened.

"Look, I get it," he said. "Eric was a cheat, a deadbeat dad. An all-around creep. Everyone in town knows it. To top it off, he got thrown in jail last weekend when he was supposed to have the kids. Or at least, that's what I heard. I understand why you would rage out over his behavior, toward both you and your kids. You went over to his place to have it out with him and, well, the rage just took over. You grabbed a knife and stabbed him, over and over and over. Problem solved. Anybody would have done the same. Especially when dealing with *your* ex."

Over and over and…? *Oh, Eric. I'm so, so sorry.* She'd loved the man once upon a time, and even now, when he truly was a deadbeat, he didn't deserve to die in such an agonizing way.

She remembered where she was, who she was with, and then it dawned on her. Dave didn't have the power here. She did. She folded her arms across her chest. "I think you've made a mistake, Detective Sanders."

"Oh yeah? And what's that?"

A sense of satisfaction washed over her. "I voluntarily came in to answer questions. But you're treating me like a suspect, and you've turned this into an interrogation. All without reading me the Miranda warning.

I'm not saying another word without a lawyer present."

Rachel glared at him, her mouth set in a tight line.

Dave's jaw clenched, and his hands gripped the table edges until his knuckles whitened.

Who's the one with an anger problem now, Dave? It wasn't like her to be petty. Still, she enjoyed getting him riled after the way he'd treated her.

Finally, he stood and jammed his chair up against the table. "Have it your way. I hope you like the orange jumpsuit you'll be wearing for the next thirty or forty years." And he stormed out.

His threat was highly effective. The moment the door slammed behind him, she began to shake. *What would my children do with both parents gone?*

No. That was not going to happen. *I'm innocent.* Taking deep, slow breaths, she calmed herself. True, she didn't have a lawyer, but she could get one. For free, if need be. Maybe not the best one, but again, she wasn't the person they were looking for. That person, the murderer, was still out there somewhere. The disquieting thought hadn't occurred to her before.

She folded her shaking hands in her lap and stared across the room. A black splotch on the wall caught her attention, and she focused on it. Sitting stone-still except for her shaking hands and hammering heart, she stared at that spot as she tried to numb her mind to Dave's authoritative blows. But it was pointless.

In agitation, she rose and paced the perimeter of the room. Over and over, back and forth, attempting to burn off some of her nervous energy. Worry for her kids invaded her mind like earwigs eating their way through her brain. She hadn't told her mom where she was going, and she had no idea how long she'd be stuck in the tiny space.

"To hell with this." She'd done her bit. If anyone else wanted to talk to her, they could come with a warrant. She reached for the door of the interrogation room, planning to walk out the same way she came in: voluntarily.

She'd had enough of what passed for justice in Resolute for one day.

ADAM WALKED INTO the interrogation room carrying two bottles of water and collided full force with Rachel. "Oof."

The bottles flew out of his hand, and he juggled them like a circus clown trying to catch them. One hit the floor, bounced twice, rolled under the table. He held out the other to Rachel. "Helen said you asked for water a while ago. When she got back to her desk and you were gone, she thought you'd left."

She stepped away as if scalded, leaving only a subtle, feminine fragrance behind that teased his senses. "Then, how did you know I was in here?"

Her about-face reaction for no apparent reason stung him. Before leaving her house earlier, he had reassured her this interview was routine, and she'd seemed fine. Well, fine considering the circumstances.

"Helen told me, after Dave told her he put you in here to wait for me."

"And now you're here for round two, I suppose." She raised her chin, almost as if challenging him.

The investigation was only hours old and already proving to be far from normal for him, even for a homicide. Helen had been right to talk to him about staying objective. He couldn't let his emotions, his feelings for Rachel, cloud his judgment. And his confusion was growing.

"Round two?" He held out the water to her again.

Rachel took the bottle, looked into Adam's eyes and burst into tears. "You…you think I k-killed him, don't you? You're all trying to find evidence to send me to prison. To take my kids away from me."

That fast, Rachel's anguish smothered whatever dispassion he'd fooled himself into believing. Adam led her to the chair on the far side of the table. "Rachel, no one's trying to take your kids, and no one, least of all me, thinks you killed your ex-husband. That's not why I asked you to come in. This is nothing more than routine questioning. Standard operating procedure."

"Really?" Even her red-rimmed eyes, puffy from crying, couldn't dim her beauty.

"Yes, really. What made you think otherwise?"

"Dave." She blurted the name. "He was horrible. He straight-out accused me, and he did it without even giving me the Miranda warning."

Adam muttered a curse under his breath. When Cassie came back from her honeymoon, the two of them were going to have a serious conversation about Dave's future in Boone County.

He grabbed a box of tissues from a shelf and set it in front of Rachel, then took the chair across from her. "Dave had no business being in here with you, and I'll make sure he knows that. On behalf of the department, I apologize for his behavior. And at the risk of sounding like a broken record, let me repeat, I have no reason to suspect you murdered Eric." He left *yet* unspoken and felt like a jerk for even thinking it. But it was his job to think it, as Helen had hammered home.

Rachel's tears slowed, her sobs becoming occasional hiccups. "Maybe deep down, I knew that. But I keep doubting my own thoughts and decisions, which is unusual for me. It's just… It's been an emotional day, and it's barely half over."

He smiled in understanding. "It has been." Now that she appeared calmer, he relaxed in his seat. "Listen, I know you're upset, but are you up to answering a few routine questions?"

She nodded, her lips curling in a hint of a return smile.

"Good." He set a recorder on the table and poised one finger over the Record button. "You okay with this?"

She shrugged, then nodded. "Wait. Before we start, can I ask you something, and you promise to tell me the truth?"

With her wide, trusting eyes staring into his, he couldn't refuse. "You can ask me anything. I may not be able to answer you, but I promise whatever I tell you will always be the truth. Good enough?"

She gave his reply a moment of consideration. "Good enough."

"Then, ask away."

"Okay. If you were me and you were in my situation, would you ask for a lawyer?"

That presented him with a conundrum. In most instances, his answer would be *yes*, getting a lawyer was a wise thing to do. But this wasn't most instances. He didn't want her lawyering up. He wanted her talking. To him. About everything in life, not just this case.

Ah, Helen. I can't do it. Objectivity in regard to Rachel simply wasn't in the cards for him. But he wasn't about to abandon his professionalism.

"When being questioned in a criminal investigation, having a lawyer is never a bad idea."

A look of panic flashed across her face. The cost of retaining counsel for the single mom of two most likely terrified her.

"But here's the thing. If at any time you want to stop the interview, you can ask for a lawyer. As soon as you do, we can't talk to you without your attorney present." He hoped she would answer all the questions now and prove herself innocent once and for all. "You think you can trust me enough to at least start the interview?"

Again, she considered his words, then nodded, and Adam felt a flood of gratification that despite her experience with Eric, she was willing to trust him, a man she knew only superficially.

"Good." He pressed the Record button. "Now then, starting this past Monday, can you give me a walk-through of your week? Days and times you worked. What you did during your time off. How you spent your evenings."

The autopsy would provide a tighter window of time when the murder had occurred, but for now Adam had to consider the entire week. When the time of death was pinned down, he'd verify Rachel's timeline and confirm her alibi as quickly as possible.

As Rachel worked her way through each day's schedule in detail, Adam jotted down notes for a working copy to keep with him. Each time he glanced up, her expression was open and guileless. If she recalled something she hadn't mentioned, she backed up to the appropriate day and had him add it to his notes.

True, the spouse must always be considered. But on the flip side, no way was Rachel the perp. And he'd do whatever was necessary—this side of the law—to ease her anxiety and clear her of the crime.

Shut down emotionally? Stay objective? *Riiight.*

THAT EVENING, Rachel and her mother were in the main house, cleaning up the dinner dishes. Daisy and Brad, tucked in for the night in the big-boy bed and the crib that her mom kept for them, were blessedly silent. Plates clinked as they were put away, and the grandfather clock in the front hallway ticked away the seconds, but otherwise, the house was quiet.

Rachel washed the last glass, handed it to her mom, then reached for a plate. Rachel loved her mother. Her mom was her best friend, closest confidante and biggest supporter. Rachel usually found comfort in the simple act of being with her, performing mundane chores together.

Eric's murder put an end to that.

At least Adam had calmed her primary concerns, though bawling like a baby in front of him today still embarrassed her. She scoffed. She couldn't begin to imagine what he must think of her, but she'd bet money it wasn't much. How could it be? Besides drop-dead gorgeous, he was quiet, always seeming to be contemplating deep thoughts. Filled to the eyebrows with integrity, trustworthy, she hoped, and let's not forget gainfully employed. What girl wouldn't hanker for him?

But he never seemed much interested in her. Polite, sure. But never more than surface friendliness. Truth be told, he never seemed much interested in anyone. Not for very long, anyway. Not that she kept up with his love life. But Resolute was a small town. People talked. And no one more than Marge.

Marge had told her more than once that Adam had a thing for her. Rachel shook her head as she washed the salad bowl. Marge was seldom wrong, but she sure as heck was wrong about this.

Pushing thoughts of Adam from her mind, Rachel tried relaxing into the quiet kitchen routine, when her mother flipped the drying towel over the edge of the sink.

"Leave the rest. The pots can soak overnight. I'll get to them in the morning."

"Done," Rachel agreed.

"How about we sit on the patio? It's a nice night. I'll mix us each a gin and tonic, and you grab the baby monitor."

"Done and done." Rachel's full-belly contentedness was starting to give way to the horrors of the day, and a drink seemed as good a remedy as anything.

Of course, her mother knew about Eric's murder. Everyone in Resolute did by now. But she didn't know all the details. As the alcohol warmed her insides and loosened her tongue, Rachel relayed her ordeal at the justice center, including her breakdown in front of Adam.

"The very idea that anyone could think you committed such a vile act is utterly ridiculous. I never realized that Dave Sanders was such a jackass."

Rachel gave a bark of laughter. "Language, Mother."

"Am I wrong?"

"No, but that's not the point. I don't need Brad's next new word to be *jackass*."

"If it is, he didn't hear it from me." The ice in her mom's glass clinked as she took a sip. "But it sure enough sounds like you put that jackass in his place."

"Maybe, but it was Adam who—"

"Made you feel better about things?"

"He did." And less scared.

"Do you trust him? I mean, what he said about the lawyer and all."

"Yes, I do. Do you think that's strange?"

"I think you should go with your gut."

Rachel gave her mother a sideways look. "You mean the gut that couldn't see what a jerk Eric was? The same gut that's all knotted up over his murder? You mean I should trust that gut?"

"If you'll remember, your gut *did* tell you about Eric. It's just that your young, hormonal self ignored the warnings." She reached over and patted Rachel's arm. "Anyone would have broken down after what you've been through today. Don't sell your gut short. Don't sell *yourself* short."

"Thanks, Mom." Rachel rested her hand on her mother's, relishing their close relationship. Divorced when Rachel was only twelve, her mom knew the rigors of single parenthood.

"So do you have any idea who might have done this to Eric? Or why?"

Rachel remained silent.

"If you don't want to talk about it, I understand."

"No, it's okay. Avoiding the subject doesn't make it go away. I've been racking my brain, but nothing is coming to mind. Sure, he hangs with some shady types, but he's been doing that for years. Do I think one of them might have killed him?" Rachel shrugged. "Maybe. But why do it now?" She sipped her drink, then glanced at the baby monitor.

"Is there something else bothering you? Besides the obvious, I mean."

Rachel sighed. "Mom, how am I going to tell the kids their daddy's gone?"

"Daisy is too young to understand right now, and I would simply tell Brad he's in heaven."

Rachel blew a raspberry.

"It's not a lie. He could be in heaven for all we know."

A companionable silence took over. The night-blackened sky filled with countless glittering stars. Hundreds of frogs chirped, and the warm air filled with the sweet scent of lavender, blooming early in her mother's yard.

Rachel startled when her mom touched her arm.

"It's getting late. I think we should head in."

Confused for a moment, Rachel realized she'd dozed

off. "Yep, we can stick a fork in this day. It needs to be done. And tomorrow I'm back at work." Rachel stood and stretched her back. "I better get some shut-eye."

"Leave the kids. They're still sleeping. You go soak those aching muscles in a steaming tub." Her mom rose and gave her one last hug. "I love you, sweetheart."

"Love you, too, Mom."

Still wrapped in the lethargy of her catnap, Rachel ambled across the lawn to the garage, digging her toes into the cool St. Augustine grass and inhaling the sultry scent of night-blooming jasmine. Her mom was right, as usual. A hot bath and a good book sounded like the right prescription to take her mind to another place.

Climbing the stairs to her apartment, she thought she heard a noise. Goose bumps covered her arms, sending chills up her spine. Standing still, she listened, finally deciding it must have been her imagination.

Nerves. That's all this was. The day had her on edge. Someone had murdered Eric and was still out there, so she was letting ordinary things spook her.

But her mother had just told her to trust her gut. Rachel pulled her phone from her pocket and tapped Adam's name in her contacts. If things went south, why not be ready to call him?

Why not be ready to call him? Because it wasn't like her to need to rely on a man, even one as solid as Adam. Not after the monumental mistake she'd made with her ex. She could take care of herself. She'd just hang on to the phone since it was already in her hand.

She continued up the stairs, reaching her front door

and turning the knob. The door creaked open. The light she always left on was out.

Don't freak out. Nothing more than a burned-out bulb.

She took one cautious step inside before a dark figure slammed into her. Air whooshed from her lungs as she spun backward onto the small landing, her back smashing into the railing. Someone ran past her and down the stairs. She cried out in pain, ricocheting toward the same steps.

Oh my God.

Her arms flailed in a futile attempt to grab the handrail. Instead, the wooden balusters she managed to wrap her fingers around wrenched her shoulders but did little to stop her downward spiral. Amid a shriek coming from her own throat, she landed at the bottom with a sickening thud, smacking her head on the concrete landing.

Darkness closed in on her as she lay there, hoping this horrible day was really over this time.

Chapter Four

The Boone County Sheriff's Office at ten o'clock on a Friday night was a quiet place. Families were tucked away in their homes, drunks were not yet intoxicated enough to cause havoc, and petty criminals were still hiding in the shadows. Just another dull night in Resolute, Texas.

Except for the Eric Miller murder investigation.

That was going to bite into Adam's time in a big way. With the justice center quiet as a tomb just now, it made sense for him to stay late and clear his desk.

Deputy Brianna Delgado had pulled the duty rotation for this weekend, but she was currently out on patrol. Their latest hire, Bree had come along at just the right time for the department. And for Noah.

Adam shook his head. Imagine Noah reeling in someone like Bree. She kept his little brother on his toes, that was for sure, but she was good for him. And apparently, he was good for her, too. They complemented each other.

First, Cassie and Bishop.

Then, Noah and Bree.

Two Reeds down, two to go.

Nate would be next.

Because, as anyone close to Adam knew—hell, the whole damn town seemed to know—Adam appeared to be eternally trapped in an unrequited infatuation hell. He rolled his head, groaning in relief when the vertebrae in his neck popped, easing some of his tension. He was beat. Time to head home.

Shutting down his computer and locking away his case files, Adam looked forward to relaxing with his feet up, two fingers of whiskey in a glass and a book open on his lap. Heaven, pure heaven.

As he locked the building's front door, his cell phone vibrated in his pocket. For an instant he considered ignoring it. Nothing good came from a call this late. But a quick glance at the display showed Rachel's name. His heart kicked up.

"Hi, Rachel."

"Adam? Oh, thank goodness. This is Martina, Rachel's mom." Her voice broke on a sob. "S-something awful has happened." More sobbing.

Adam's chest tightened.

"Need you…to get to the house right away. Rachel… There's blood everywhere." Despite her broken sentences, interspersed with sobs, the message came through loud and clear.

Adam full out ran to his cruiser, the tightening in his chest ramping up to a sharp, stabbing pain. "Martina? Martina! Can you hear me?"

"Y-y-yes."

"Good. Have you called 9-1-1?"

"I called them first. Hurry, Adam. Please hurry. My baby's not moving. I think…" She broke down in sobs again.

Adam's insides turned stone-cold. "I'm on my way." He hopped in his cruiser, flipped on the lights and siren, burning rubber as he squealed out of the parking lot and raced to the north side of town.

Please be okay. Please be okay. He repeated the three words like a mantra the entire way.

After six and a half minutes that felt more like six hours, he rammed his vehicle's tires against the curb in front of the Novotnys' house. Red flashing lights from the ambulance punctuated the night like stab wounds and fed his fear.

Out of his cruiser in an instant, he charged up the long drive to the garage. Two paramedics, one crouched on each side of a backboard, glanced up as his shadow fell across them.

Adam looked down and stopped breathing. It took him several agonizing seconds to realize what he was seeing. Rachel was being strapped to the board, not zipped into a body bag. Unconscious, not dead. He released his breath.

She wore a neck stabilizer. Standard precaution for back and neck injuries. But Lord have mercy, she looked so small, so helpless, so pale.

Except where angry, red lacerations crisscrossed her arms and hands. Her long blond hair, now red from the bleeding gash on her head, trailed across her shoulders in sticky clumps. The top half of her shirt appeared wet and black.

So much blood. Her blood.

Adam's fear boiled into anger, and the raw emotion caused an unfamiliar rasp in his voice. "How is she?"

Prizzy, the female half of the paramedic team, straightened to her full height somewhere north of six feet. Her dark hair hung to her waist in a thick braid. "Vitals are good. But the head injury is severe. We need to transport her right away."

"Concussion for sure." Jeff, the other paramedic, assisted Prizzy in moving the backboard onto a stretcher.

Wishing Rachel would open her eyes, Adam walked alongside as they wheeled the stretcher to the rear of the ambulance. Brain injuries, especially where there was a loss of consciousness, were serious, potentially debilitating.

Please be okay.

"Adam! Thank goodness you came." Martina hustled up the drive and gave him a tight hug. When she stepped back and looked at him, her red-rimmed eyes were puffy, but anger lurked in the depths as well. "I saw someone running across the property right after she screamed. Find out who did this to my baby. Lock him up and throw away the key."

"Count on it."

"I'm holding you to that." Then she turned to the paramedics. "Can I ride to the hospital with her?"

From across the stretcher, Prizzy glanced at the distraught woman. "Of course. You can buckle up with me in the front."

Once Rachel was secured in the ambulance, Jeff

hopped inside and began hooking up an IV. Martina and Prizzy got into the front.

Before she shut the ambulance door, Adam reached for Martina's arm to stop her. "What about Rachel's kids?" He scanned the small crowd of concerned neighbors, searching for someone with a little boy and a baby.

Rachel's mom laid her hand on Adam's cheek, shocking him with the power of that maternal gesture. "You're sweet to remember the children. Missy Jenkins lives in the next house down, my side of the street. She's keeping them at her house, but she's got a key to my place in case she needs anything. I've got Marge's cell number. I'll call her when I get to the hospital, tell her Rachel won't be at work tomorrow."

"Looks like you have things well in hand. I'll be at the hospital as soon as I'm done here."

"I see why Rachel thinks so highly of you." Tears rolled down her face, and she held a tissue to her nose as Adam closed the door.

Adam had a hard time believing Rachel thought about him at all, but he gave her mother what he hoped was a reassuring smile before the ambulance drove away, lights blaring and siren wailing. Why did it feel like his heart was being driven away in that vehicle?

He walked over to the group of neighbors who'd gathered outside, some in their pajamas, to watch the goings-on. He conducted cursory interviews, had them all write their name, address and phone number on a piece of paper. But none of them had seen anyone running away from Rachel's home, and only one had heard her scream. They'd mostly come outside because of the ambulance. One by one, they dispersed back to their beds.

Adam rounded the side of the garage. A viscous puddle of blood at the base of the stairs caused his gut to tighten. He slipped a pair of paper booties over his shoes, then forced his hands, clammy from the humid night air, into a pair of nitrile gloves. The bottom few steps bore drops and smudges of blood, which he photographed.

Working his way up the wooden stairs with his tactical flashlight, he found and photographed where Rachel had hit her head. Or rather, one of the spots. One corner of a square baluster was splintered and covered in blood. Several strands of long blond hair twisted around a protruding sliver and fluttered in the slight breeze.

Adam noticed two more places along the handrail smeared with blood. Looked like Rachel had tried to grab hold as she fell, scraping herself up. Or possibly the intruder injured himself while fleeing, but he doubted they'd been that lucky. Still, he bagged and tagged the scrapings, hoping DNA might identify the perp.

He reached the top landing and pushed on the partially open door. It swung farther into the pitch-black apartment. Leaning in, Adam used the end of his tactical light to tap a wall switch into its upward position. An overhead light came on, revealing a mess similar to the one he'd found in Eric's apartment. Throw pillows ripped apart. Couch and chair cushions slashed.

Everything that had been in a drawer now on counters, tabletops or the floor.

On his drive over, Adam hadn't wanted to draw a line between what happened to Rachel and what had happened to Eric. But now? It seemed a strong possibility that the same person had searched both apartments, and that person had possibly killed Eric as well. If so, Rachel was lucky to have escaped with her life, and that chilled him to the bone.

Footsteps sounded on the outside stairs, and Adam, already angry and on edge, pushed his back against the wall and drew his gun. Perps often returned to the scene of the crime, especially if they'd been interrupted.

Bree called out before entering. "Adam, if you're in there, I'm coming in."

Adam released the breath he'd been holding and holstered his weapon. "Come ahead." He was glad she was on call. Since coming on board a few months ago, Bree had already earned the reputation for having the sharpest eye for detail in the department.

"Sorry it took me a while to get here. There was another free-for-all at the Dead End. I called Dave in to help transport the miscreants to their six-by-nine concrete weekend getaway." Bree gave Adam an assessing once over. "You okay?"

He shrugged. "Hard when you know the people involved."

"Isn't that pretty much always the case in Resolute?"

He gave her a feeble grin. "Pretty much."

"So it's the fact that it's Rachel, then?"

"Pretty much," he admitted, relieved when she pushed him no further on that score.

Already wearing booties, Bree pulled on gloves as she surveyed the apartment. "The 9-1-1 call said Rachel fell down the stairs. Her mother thinks she saw someone. I already saw the blood and damage on my way up. You want me to start processing outside?"

In the short time since Bree had rolled into town, she and Rachel had become close, yet somehow Bree maintained a professional detachment in the face of her friend's assault that Adam seemed incapable of. He admired her for that.

"No, I've already started processing outside. Also got names and numbers from the neighbors, not that they'll be much use. You can start processing in here."

"Will do." She met Adam's eyes and raised her brows. "Anything to add?"

Adam shook his head. "I'll finish up outside, then head to the hospital to interview Martina. Rachel, too, if she's awake." Officially, he'd question Rachel. Unofficially, he wanted—no, he needed—to make sure she was all right before he lost his ever-loving mind.

"Works for me." Still standing in the doorway, Bree took another look at the mess. "So tell me, boss, is this my case? Or you think it's related to her ex's murder?"

"Mighty big coincidence if they weren't related, so unless we find definitive proof otherwise, I'm treating them as connected cases. So, my case. But you'll work it with me."

"Me? Not your brother?" She fought a smile, her words carrying a tone of barely disguised enthusiasm.

And a big helping of competitiveness. Those two, always trying to one-up each other.

"You're the one who caught the call. Besides, I've got something else in mind for Noah."

They worked in silence, Adam outside, Bree inside, until he bagged the last piece of evidence and glanced at his watch. He peeled off his gloves and called out. "Hey, rookie?"

From inside, Bree hollered back. "I'm no rookie, old man."

"Yeah, yeah. Call me when you've finished processing the scene. Let me know if you find anything interesting."

"Will do. And, Adam?"

He looked up to find Bree standing on the landing above his head. "Yeah?"

"If you talk to Rachel, give her my love."

He gave Bree a curt nod and left. As he jogged to his cruiser, the mantra began again.

Please be okay. Please be okay.

ADAM HUSTLED THROUGH the hospital's emergency-room entrance, past a triage area and up to the ER receptionist's desk.

"Octavia, I'm looking for Rachel Miller." Between injured family members, deputies and arrestees, he knew the ER receptionist well.

"She's in bed seven, but— Adam, wait," she called out when he took off at a run. He slid to a stop and faced her. "She's not there right now. They took her upstairs for tests." She favored him with a sympathetic smile.

"Her mother is still in there, and I think she could use a little company."

Massaging the back of his neck with one hand, Adam nodded. Striving for a disciplined, professional image, he walked, not ran, past the row of curtains to the one next to last and pulled it open. Martina sat on a hard plastic chair, elbows on her knees, face in her hands. At the sound of the curtain rings sliding along the metal rod, she looked up and swiped away tears.

He pulled the curtain closed again and squatted next to her chair. "How are you doing?"

Rachel's mom sat up, though her shoulders remained hunched forward. Lips pressed in a firm line, she wrung her hands. When she glanced up at him, she simply shook her head as more tears trailed down her ashen face.

Adam's professional demeanor vanished. "Rachel?"

Martina shrugged. "I don't know. They took her for a CT scan. To assess possible brain damage. Oh, Adam, what if—"

"No what-ifs. We wait to hear what the doctor has to say, okay?"

She brushed away her tears and gave him an affirmative nod. "You're right. I've had way too much time to think, and I'm imagining all kinds of terrible scenarios."

"Well, I'm here now. And I make for a pretty good distraction."

"Thank you. I can't tell you how much your being here means to me."

Before he could reply, the curtain slid open again,

and Octavia entered, carrying another visitor's chair. "Figured you could use something to sit on while you wait."

"Thanks." Adam straightened up and took the chair.

"Can you tell me if Rachel will be coming back here, or will she be admitted?" Martina asked.

"The doctor will make that determination, but you're welcome to wait in here unless we need the bed." Holding the curtain back, Octavia paused before closing it. "If she's admitted, Mrs. Novotny, I'll get you the room number. In the meantime, if either of you would like anything, just ask. Coffee, bottles of water, anything."

Rachel's mother shook her head.

After Octavia left, Adam said, "See? She might not even be admitted." His words sounded lame even to his own ears. "You'll see, Martina. She'll be fine."

Her brows knitted together. "Will you tell me something?"

"Anything." He put his chair next to hers and settled into it, his stomach churning at the sight of a small blood stain on his uniform's sleeve.

"Tell me how Rachel wound up at the bottom of the stairs. Did she fall or was she pushed?"

And this was always the fine line law enforcement walked. What to tell the families without compromising an open investigation. "Nothing is conclusive at this point, but no, I don't think Rachel fell on her own. Someone broke into her apartment."

"Are you sure?"

Adam nodded. "I think she might have surprised

him, since you saw someone running away. He may have pushed her or just bumped into her as he was trying to escape."

"You think it was a man?"

He pulled his notepad and pen from his shirt pocket. "You tell me. You're the only one, besides Rachel, who saw anything."

Martina dropped her forehead into her hand. "It happened so fast, and it was dark. I'm just not sure."

"I know this is hard for you. Just take your time, and walk me through your evening."

She pulled a tissue from the sleeve of her sweater and dabbed at her nose, then told Adam about their night. Putting the kids to bed, having dinner, retiring to the patio. Martina picked up a water bottle from the floor next to her chair and took a sip.

"When I noticed she could barely keep her eyes open, I told her to leave the kids with me for the night. They were already asleep, and I had grabbed the diaper bag from her place earlier, so I shooed her home." She took a deep breath. "It was my fault. I sent her into danger." With a shaking hand holding her bottle, she sipped more water.

Adam gripped her forearms. "It was not your fault. Do you hear me?"

She looked him square in the eyes. "In my mind, I know it. My heart is a different creature. I saw her start up the stairs, and I keep thinking if only I had waited, just a bit longer, I might have..." She shook her head. "Instead, I collected our glasses and the baby monitor and headed back inside to check on the kids."

Her eyes dropped. "I'd just walked into their room when I heard a god-awful commotion. Thumping and thudding and—" she inhaled a jerky breath "—Rachel screaming. I will never forget that sound as long as I live. Sent instant chills racing up and down my spine. Then there was nothing." She paused, her lower lip trembling. "The silence was a hundred times worse. I ran out the back door toward the garage. Halfway there I saw a dark shape hightailing it around the front corner of the house."

"Do you remember anything more about the person? Any details at all?"

Martina thought for a moment. "I couldn't see his face, but I think it was a man. Too broad to be a woman. Not very tall, either, but fast, or so it seemed to me. Dressed in dark clothes, maybe a hoodie, but I was focused on Rachel. My baby was lying at the bottom of the steps, bleeding. Oh Lord, there was so much blood." She caught her breath and began sobbing again.

Adam cleared his throat. "Take your time."

Rachel's mom pulled back on the waterworks and went on. "I'd left my phone in the house, but hers was lying on the ground. I called 9-1-1 first, then you."

His curiosity getting the best of him, he met her gaze. "Why did you call me after 9-1-1?" The emergency call would've been dispersed to the fire department, ambulance and sheriff's office.

"Well, I mean, I thought 9-1-1 would bring an ambulance faster." She twisted her tissue into shreds. "Was I supposed to have called you first?"

"No, I didn't mean that." He shouldn't have even

asked her. It wasn't the right time. "I just meant, why did you call me at all?"

"Oh. Well, you were already pulled up in her contacts and—" she rested a hand on his and gave him a small smile "—I just thought you'd want to know."

Before he could react, the metal curtain loops slid along the rod again. "Rachel's been taken to a room." Octavia handed a piece of paper with the room number on it to Martina, who glanced at it, then passed it to Adam.

"Thanks, Octavia." Adam stood. "You hear anything on her condition?"

"I'm sure the doctor will talk with Martina in Rachel's room after he's gone over the scans."

Adam forced himself to shorten his stride and stick to Martina's pace as he escorted her to her daughter's room. For Martina's sake, he tried to stay positive and ignore the ominous thoughts fighting for his attention. But his brain buzzed with anxiety.

Please be okay, Rachel. Please be okay.

ADAM FOLLOWED MARTINA exactly three steps into Rachel's hospital room before his feet froze in place. Rachel lay still as death, her eyes closed. Her head was bandaged and wrapped in gauze. Dark bruises on her forehead and near her left eye disappeared beneath the dressings. Her arms rested on top of a thin hospital blanket, the scratches and scrapes he'd seen earlier standing out starkly against her pale skin. The sight of her grabbed his heart and squeezed until he couldn't breathe.

Martina rushed to her daughter's bedside and grasped

her hand, oblivious to his distress. Equally oblivious was the nurse in the room, busy adjusting a drip bag and updating the portable patient monitor.

Adam stepped closer, the abrasions on Rachel's chin and cheeks becoming more noticeable beneath a layer of ointment. The slight rise and fall of her chest and the steady beep from the EKG machine told him she was alive, even if she barely looked it.

His fingers twitched, eager to curl into fists. The rush of blood in his ears blocked out the voice of reason. *I'm going to find the bastard who did this and—*

"Adam?" Martina put her hand on his shoulder. "The doctor's here."

He blinked to awareness, motivated by his renewed resolve. At some point the nurse had left, and Adam took in the middle-aged man wearing green scrubs who stood before them.

"I'm Dr. Mason." He glanced at Adam but aimed his words at Martina. "May I speak freely in front of the deputy?"

"Of course."

"Ms. Miller suffered a grade-two concussion. The good news is, the CT scan revealed no brain bleeds or clots." He glanced at the wall clock, which showed they'd segued into early Saturday morning. "I'd like to keep her today for observation, but if everything looks good, we'll probably release her this evening. Tomorrow morning at the latest."

Martina's hand flew to her chest. "Thank God. What about her other injuries?"

"No broken bones or internal injuries. Plenty of lacerations, but none that won't heal with minimum care. Her head wound's been stitched. The nurse will give you instructions for home care when she's released." Dr. Mason patted Martina's shoulder. "Your daughter's very lucky." He took a step toward the door.

Adam stopped him. "If nothing major is wrong with her, why is she still unconscious?"

"She's not. Ms. Miller had a panic attack while we were getting her ready for her scan. That can be a side effect of her head injury. We gave her a mild sedative that doesn't cause complications with concussions." The doctor smiled. "Between that and her adrenaline drop, she'll likely sleep through the night. Any other questions?" Adam shook his head, and the doctor added, "If you have any that the nurse can't answer, have her page me. I'll be in to see Rachel later this morning when she's awake."

"Thank you, Doctor," Martina said, her relief palpable. After he left, she moved to the far side of the bed and stared down at Rachel. "When I first saw her, crumpled up at the bottom of the stairs, I thought she was dead." Tears crept down her cheeks. "I wonder why people are always so quick to think the worst."

Adam pulled a visitor's chair closer to the bed and sat. "I don't understand how Rachel could have a panic attack if she was unconscious in the scan room."

Martina's eyes widened. "Oh, sorry. I forgot to mention it. She regained consciousness in the ambulance. The EMT with her in the back told Prizzy and me through the speaker that she opened her eyes and looked around but didn't say anything."

Adam nodded. It would have been nice to know, but he didn't blame Rachel's mom for the memory lapse. As upset as *he* was, he couldn't imagine the level of distress Martina was experiencing.

Except, I can. Sort of.

He'd never had to sit vigil in a hospital, waiting to find out if a loved one was going to die or wake up from a severe head injury. For him, it had been the stunned attempt to accept that his father's bullet-ridden body would be Adam's last memory of him.

And long before that, he'd had to force his ten-year-old brain to absorb the sorrow of losing his mother. Deal with his rage toward her when one day she'd just walked away, leaving them all behind.

Adam looked at Martina, her exhaustion evident in the dark circles beneath her puffy eyes, her drooping shoulders, the curve in her spine. "You heard the doctor, she'll be out for hours. Why don't you head home and get some rest? I can stay here tonight."

"I appreciate it, but I'd like to spend tonight here with her. I *would* like to run home, get a few things I need, check on the kids. Could you stay with Rachel until I get back?"

"Of course. Take your time."

On her way past him to the door, Martina patted his shoulder. "You're a good man, Adam Reed."

A few minutes later, his phone dinged with a text from Bree.

Found something, might be interesting. Details tomorrow morning.

He replied with a thumbs-up emoji and muted his phone.

In the dimly lit room, its silence broken only by rhythmic mechanical beeps, Adam again watched Rachel's chest rise and fall in a steady proof of life. Her battered face looked almost peaceful as she slept. He reached for her hand and held it, careful to avoid the bandaged scrapes. "I'm going to find the man who did this to you, and I *will* make him pay."

His thumb caressed the back of her hand, as if he could somehow infuse her with his strength, let her know that he was there. That he would do whatever was needed to keep her safe.

He wanted revenge on the person who'd hurt Rachel. But raised by his father to follow the rules, could he take the law into his own hands? Martina's words echoed in his mind. *You're a good man, Adam Reed.*

He closed his eyes, the words that flowed unbidden through his mind more of a bargain than a prayer. *If she wakes up with no long-lasting effects from the concussion, when I find the person who did this, I won't kill him.* Seemed a fair trade.

Opening his eyes, Adam stood over the woman who'd been terrorized, battered, nearly killed tonight. And in that moment, he realized the depth of his feelings for her.

His fingers twitched again, and this time he let them curl into his palms.

We'll see just how good a man I really am.

Chapter Five

The next morning Adam, blurry-eyed and fuzzy-brained, sat parked in front of Sweets and Treats, waiting for the candy and ice-cream shop to open. He rubbed his tired eyes and took another careful sip of piping hot coffee. After getting only a few hours of restless sleep, he was depending on an extra-large, extra-strong coffee from the Busy B Café to keep him alert. A special brew Marge made for Noah that Adam usually refused to drink. Not this morning.

Between his bouts of sleep, he'd worried about Rachel. His overactive mind stayed on hyperdrive, going over everything that had happened. To Eric. To Rachel. Trying to piece together the connection. But mostly, trying to figure out how he planned to keep Rachel safe.

As the eastern sky lightened beyond his bedroom window, he'd finally given up on any more shut-eye and called the hospital to check on her status. According to the charge nurse, she was still sleeping the last time they'd checked on her.

The tight band inside his chest had loosened a bit.

He'd tried to deny his feelings for Rachel ever since his return from college when he came home to find her married. Now he was having trouble dismissing them. Careful to keep them hidden from everyone, he'd admitted to himself last night that he'd never stopped caring for her.

But despite his relief from hearing the nurse's report, his brow continued to furrow with concern for Rachel. Unless last night's culprit had fled Resolute, Rachel could still be in danger. Martina and the kids, too. And because she'd interrupted the intruder, Adam's gut told him whatever the man had been searching for remained unfound.

But why search Rachel's place? He kept coming back to that question, gnawing on it like a dog with a juicy bone. Surely, she wasn't engaged in any of Eric's shadier dealings. Or was she? Was he blinded by his feelings for her?

His father had told him on more than one occasion, when in doubt, remove emotion from the equation and look at the facts. The facts were that Rachel was generally strapped for cash, supporting herself and her two small kids as a single parent working a waitressing job. Plus paying for online classes. But would she risk losing everything by stepping on the wrong side of the law?

No way. Even setting aside his feelings, he'd observed Rachel for years at the Busy B. Kind to even the whiniest customer, she stuck up for the underdog and had even volunteered to help get Bree's youth program off the ground. Rachel's boss displayed an undeniable affinity for her favorite waitress, and Marge was never wrong when it came to judging a person's character.

He glanced at the store. The Closed sign still faced out. Sandy, the store manager, didn't open the place up until ten, but with her car parked in the back alley, he knew she was already inside. Eight forty-five according to his watch. He speed-dialed the office.

"Boone County Sheriff's Department. How may I help you?" Helen's strong, clear voice answered.

"It's Adam. Why are you answering phones on a Saturday?" The department's part-time employee took over Helen's desk on her weekends off.

"Sonia's not feeling well. I told her I'd work today and tomorrow and swap two weekdays with her when she's back on her feet. And besides—" her tone perked up "—things around here are becoming too compelling. I don't want to sit home and miss all the action."

Amused by Helen's enthusiasm, Adam chuckled. "I just called to let Bree and anyone else who may be working today know that I'll be late."

"No one else is here yet, but I'll let them know when I see them." Her tone became concerned. "I read the call logs when I got in. Is Rachel all right?"

"I think so. I want to go by the hospital and check on her, see if she can answer a few questions about last night."

"Give her my love."

"I will." Adam paused. "When you do see Bree, please let her know to stick close to the office. I need to meet with her when I get in."

"You got it." She disconnected to answer another line ringing in the background.

He climbed out of his car, walked up to the front window and looked in. When he saw Sandy, he rapped on the glass.

She looked up from a display case and pointed to a wristwatch she wasn't wearing, then rolled her eyes and unlocked the door. "Geez, Adam. I know you like the occasional sweet, but waiting with your nose pressed up against the glass isn't a good look on you." Sandy turned the Closed sign to Open and sighed. "Might as well let the rest of the line in, too."

Adam glanced over his shoulder at the empty sidewalk outside, then back at Sandy. "Ah, yes. You're the one in your family with the sarcastic sense of humor."

"Absolutely not true. We're all sarcastic. But we don't all have a sense of humor, so be thankful I'm the funny one." Sandy scurried behind the front counter and continued setting up fresh truffles in a display case. "So what can I help you with? I've got a giant jawbreaker, guaranteed to keep Noah from talking for two days."

Adam smiled at that but shook his head.

"No? How about some taffy that'll tucker out your jaw right quick? Or lemon drops—"

Walking past the small area of bistro tables and chairs along the right-hand side of the shop, Adam interrupted her before she continued making suggestions. "Thanks, but no. I need a bag of those nugget-sized peanut butter and coconut candies."

"Interesting fact. Did you know they're made in east

Texas?" The redhead pointed toward the row of bins stacked three high, attached to the left wall. "Somewhere in the middle of the row, bottom bin. I'd show you, but I've gotta finish my preopening routine which was so rudely interrupted." She laughed. "And use the scoop, even if they *are* wrapped in plastic. I'm still recovering from that idiot who ran his filthy hands through all the loose candy a few months ago."

Adam pulled a plastic bag from a roll similar to produce bags in the supermarket and began filling it with the scoop.

"Better watch how many you take, Deputy." Sandy's eyes met his over the truffle tower she was building. "That there's a cavity-causing candy if ever there was one."

"They're not for me."

Sandy looked up, her eyebrows angling skyward. "Okay…but they must be for someone special since you practically bulldozed your way in here. An hour before opening, I might add. So spill it."

He wasn't keen on becoming fodder for the gossip mill any more than he already might be, but he did owe her for opening up early. "They're for Brad Miller, Rachel's son." He kept his tone nonchalant, as if it were just a normal duty for the town's chief deputy to buy candy for someone's kid.

"Okay, I can't tease you on that one. Poor tyke could probably use a double dose of anything that makes him feel better, what with his daddy getting himself killed like that." Sandy turned around and flipped open the ice-cream coolers' lids to check the tubs. "I never did understand what she saw in that guy. Back when we were all in high school together, she could've had any boy she wanted."

The bell on the door tinkled, but Adam remained facing the wall, focused on scooping the orange crunchy candies into his bag.

"Told ya, Nate. Our bro's got a bigger sweet tooth than you and I combined. Bet he keeps 'em locked in his chief deputy's desk in his chief deputy's office with the always-closed chief deputy's door."

Adam groaned. Nothing like having to deal with his twin brothers when he was running on empty. He turned around to see both younger siblings wearing cat-ate-the-canary grins, although that's where any similarity between the two ended.

"Seriously, dude." Nate shook his head. "You're never gonna find a woman if all your teeth rot and fall out."

"Haven't seen you doing much dating since you came back from California, *Nathaniel*." Adam smirked. Nate hated it when anyone called him by his full first name. Funny how it worked with siblings. You never quite outgrew the teasing and taunting. "And that was, what? About a year ago?"

It had been a silly thing to say. Adam knew it the second the words left his mouth. All three Reeds sobered, and a heavy silence descended. Nate had come home for their father's funeral, and the reminder was still heart-wrenching.

"With his fancy security business out there on the West Coast, I bet Nate's dance card is filled with Hollywood starlets and socialites," Sandy butted in, lightening the mood. She turned to the twins. "And by the way, what are you two doing in here? The store's not even open yet."

"All evidence to the contrary. Open sign in the window, a customer inside." Nate shrugged.

"Nate and I were just on our way to breakfast when we saw Adam through the front window and decided to say hi." Noah, the most lighthearted one in the family, snickered. "Thought maybe you were getting something to take to Rachel in the hospital."

Adam let out a frustrated sigh at Noah's implication. Apparently, his efforts to keep his interest in Rachel on the down-low hadn't fooled his brothers.

"What?" Sandy's normally loud voice reached a new octave as she glared at Adam. "Why is Rachel in the hospital? And why didn't you tell me first thing when you got here?"

Adam figured he might as well tell her, since the whole town would know soon enough. And best to nip exaggerated versions of the story in the bud. "Someone broke into her place last night, and she walked in on the guy when she got home. He ran out, pushing her down the stairs in the process. She's banged up pretty good and has a mild concussion."

Sandy shook her head. "Poor Rachel."

"You mean poor Adam. Our big brother's had a crush on her for darn near his whole life, so it stands to reason he'd be here, getting sweets for his sweetie." Noah only laughed when Adam gave him a hostile stare. "Come on, bro. You really think no one knows you've been crushing on her since middle school?"

"Now, Noah, be fair," Nate joined in. "Maybe we're just aware of it because he's our brother. I'm sure no one else notices him at a total loss for words whenever Rachel serves him in the diner."

"Or how he almost drools in his food as she walks away from his table," Noah said.

Sandy sauntered over next to Adam and drew her brows together as if about to cry. "Oh, Adam, how could you? I always thought—" she sniffled "—that someday you and I…would wind up together."

Adam stared at her, gobsmacked.

She put the back of one hand to her forehead. "You wicked, wicked man. You've done gone and broke my heart." Then she doubled over with laughter that seemed too big for such a petite woman.

The twins joined in. Adam didn't.

"Very funny." He closed the bin's lid and wrapped a twist tie around the top of his bag. "I may have had a crush on her back in school, but that was a long time ago. I'm sure as hell not still harboring one."

"Riiight." Noah nodded, his expression and tone not at all convincing.

"Uh-huh." Nate rolled his lips in to keep from laughing.

"I'm going to die a lonely spinster," Sandy wailed, not even trying to keep a straight face on her way back to the counter.

Adam followed her but turned to his brothers before making his purchase. "Why don't you guys go have yourselves a good laugh outside. But wait for me. I've got a special assignment for you, Noah."

The two youngest Reeds chuckled on their way to the exit.

"Ooh, you get a *special* assignment." Nate elbowed his twin.

Noah wiped tears from his eyes. "Maybe I get to babysit his soon-to-be stepkids."

The door closed on their mirth, and Adam took out his wallet.

Sandy stopped laughing, but her smile stayed locked in place. "Aren't you forgetting something?"

He set the bag on the counter.

Sandy crossed her arms and arched a brow. "You're going to visit a woman in the hospital with a bag of candy for her son and nothing for her? Crush or no crush, you need to man up. Ignore your inane brothers for once, and at least take Rachel some sort of get-well gift."

When he just stood there, struggling to form a coherent thought about gifts, Sandy rolled her eyes. She assembled a cardboard truffle box and placed a different chocolatey morsel in each of the eight divided sections. After closing the lid and locking it in place, she set the box down and plopped the bag on her scale. She rang it up, added on the truffles and took Adam's credit card.

"Now, if you're smarter than you look—and I have to admit you're the smartest-looking Reed, after Cassie, that is—you'll pop in next door and let Frannie help you pick out a nice bouquet." She bagged his purchase, handed it to him with his card and gave him a wink. "Personally, I think it's cute that you're still crushing on her. But if things don't work out with Rachel, just mosey your sweet behind right on back here, and we'll see what's what."

Adam rolled *his* eyes this time, then strode out the door, Sandy's hearty laughter following him.

Noah and Nate leaned against his SUV, grinning at him like fools.

"You really have a special assignment for me? Or did you just not want us to see you buying a box of those fancy chocolates for Rachel?" Noah asked.

Adam wrapped an arm around Noah's neck and dragged him several feet away from Nate. "I'm going to be busy with this murder, so I'd like you to take over some of my other cases." He dropped his arm. "You've been proving yourself more than capable this year, and I believe you're ready to take on additional responsibilities."

His eyes lighting up like a kid's on Christmas morning, Noah nodded. "Thanks, bro. I won't let you down." He rejoined his twin. "You hear that, Nate? Adam's going to drop everything to work on his *girlfriend's* case, so he's assigning me the rest of his files."

"But one other thing first." Adam grinned as he walked past them. "After you two have breakfast, Noah, you can patrol the north half of the county."

Noah hated patrolling and handing out traffic tickets. "Dave's already—"

"Then, you can join him. Divide the area in half, then switch halves after you each finish your own."

Noah hmphed. Nate chuckled, then the badgeless twin put his arm across his brother's shoulders and steered him toward the corner.

Adam waited to make sure they didn't turn around, then darted into Frannie's Flowers. The scent of something made him sneeze, and the deeper into the shop he ventured, the stronger it became. It was like someone had knocked over the entire shelf of discount perfumes at the general store, and he cursed his allergies.

An older woman came out from the back, her graying hair pulled back with barrettes and a kind smile on her face. "Howdy, Adam. I hope you're not here for a solemn occasion."

"No, ma'am. Not exactly."

Miss Frannie had designed and donated the casket spray and display flowers for the family when they buried their dad. She'd known Wallace Reed all his life and insisted she could do better than anything they'd pick out. Considering the collective emotional state of the family, they'd readily agreed, with gratitude.

"So…flowers for your special girl? Not that I've heard about one lately." She gave him a quick wink.

Does everybody in this town keep track of my dating life?

"I'd like to get some flowers for Rachel Miller. She had a bad fall yesterday, and I thought they might help cheer her up."

"Oh no." Her smile disappeared. "I hope she's not hurt too bad."

Adam rubbed his twitching nose. "She's in the hospital, but I think she'll recover just fine."

“Thank heavens. And it’s about time you did something proactive about that crush of yours.” She came out from behind the counter. “I swear, I thought I’d see the pearly gates before you and that girl finally got together.”

Adam bit his lip out of respect for his elders. But what the actual…?

“I can tell you’re surprised I know.” Frannie chuckled. “These peepers of mine may be getting old, but they still don’t miss much. And they didn’t miss anything back in the day. I darn near lost all hope when you went off to college and Rachel married that ne’er-do-well.”

Clearing his throat, he looked around as his nose got stuffier. “I’m not sure what to get her.”

Frannie rubbed her hands together, then walked toward the wall coolers full of bouquets and vase arrangements. “For a hospital visit, you want something cheerful that’ll brighten up the room and the patient.” She opened a cooler door, pulled out a bright arrangement and held it toward Adam, who sneezed. “Hmm, you’re right. These lilies give off a powerful smell. Lotta people don’t really like ’em.” She put it back and pulled out another one. “Now, this here one only has a little fragrance from the roses. She might like roses since they’re from you.”

Holy hell. At least now he knew to avoid lilies for the rest of his life. But roses? Way too…meaningful. His mind went back to the previous afternoon when Rachel was working in her garden. *Bouquets wither and die. But a potted plant with blooms will last for however long you care for it.* "I think she'd like a plant instead of cut flowers."

"Well, they can be nice, but to brighten up her mood," she said as she wound her way through the shop with Adam on her heels, "flower arrangements are your best bet." She stopped before a large display of potted green plants, varying from small succulent gardens on the top shelves to four-foot-tall rubber trees on the floor.

Adam scanned the area. "No, I meant a potted plant *with* flowers."

Frannie patted his arm. "Now you're talking. Perfect compromise." She grabbed his hand and led him to what he'd been looking for, even before he knew it.

After comparing several, he chose a pot loaded with blooming daisies. "I'll take this one."

"Are you sure? Look at these adorable miniature rose plants." She gave him a sly look.

"I don't want to give her roses, regardless of their size. Besides, her favorite flowers are daisies."

Frannie took the plant from him, set it down, grabbed his hand again and pulled him back to the counter. "Wait one jiff."

True to her word, she returned in seconds, holding a plant exactly like the one he'd chosen. "See?" She held it under his nose. "This one has plenty of flowers, and also lots of buds that will keep the joy coming."

"You're an angel, Miss Frannie." Adam smiled. "Will they last very long?" Even on a plant, dying flowers would be depressing.

"They sure will. After she gets home, she can keep them inside as long as she takes care of them. And

Rachel's got one heck of a green thumb. If she wants, she can plant them outside in that little garden of hers. They'll bloom twice a year without fail."

As she rang up the plant, Adam spotted two more items he wanted to get. He brought them back to the register.

He walked out of the store with a huge grin that faded the minute he turned toward his vehicle. Noah and Nate were once again leaning against it. He walked into the street to approach it from the driver's side while the twins nudged each other and made kissing noises.

"Why don't you two grow up." He opened his door, but before climbing in he added, "Noah, I'm writing you up unless you skip breakfast and head north to patrol right now."

Noah's mouth dropped open, and Nate laughed as he walked away from his twin. "Don't worry, bro, I got this," he called over his shoulder to Noah. "Just tell me what you would have ordered, and I'll eat it for you. You can pay me back later."

It was Adam's turn to laugh as he drove off, Noah in his rearview mirror with his mouth still hanging open.

Chapter Six

Beeps and whirs and antiseptic smells brought Rachel back to awareness before she opened her eyes. Hospital. Head hurt. *Everything* hurt.

Soft echoes of words in Adam's voice ricocheted in her mind. Despite her body's pain, they brought her a sense of comfort and safety, as if cocooned in a soft, thick blanket and cuddled. With her eyes still closed, she pictured him holding her in his arms, her head resting against his chest.

But indistinct voices tugged at her attention. Opening her eyes, her gaze landed on her mother, sleeping on a recliner between the bed and the room's only window.

She twisted her neck in the opposite direction, clenching her teeth against a ten-out-of-ten pain drumming a beat in her head. She'd expected to see Adam's concerned expression, but the visitor's chair sat empty, and a curious disappointment settled over her. She must have conjured him in her dreams. It wouldn't be the first time Deputy Reed had shown up there. Though, it would be the first time they were PG-rated.

Her mouth was so parched she could barely swallow. Although the top of her bed had already been raised, she found the remote fastened to the rail next to her and brought herself to an upright sitting position. Condensation dripped down the sides of a plastic cup on the tray table. She reached for it, a new pain shooting through her shoulder and arm as she got one finger on the edge. It skated on its film of water, hit the bed railing and smacked the floor, ice chips shooting in all directions.

"What? What is it?" Rachel's mom bolted upright in the recliner and scrambled to her feet, one hand on the left side of her chest when she caught sight of her daughter. "Thank heavens you're awake." She leaned over the bed to give her a hug and didn't let go.

"I'm sorry I woke you. I knocked the ice on the floor." Rachel's voice cracked like the sunbaked floor of Death Valley. "Uh, ow…you're squeezing my bruises, Mom." She twisted a little to loosen her mother's grip.

"I'd be upset if you didn't wake me. I've been waiting all night to see those beautiful big eyes." Her mother brushed a tendril of Rachel's hair away from her face. "Have you been awake long?"

Rachel shook her head and immediately regretted it. A wave of vertigo washed over her, nausea close on its heels. "No, I—" A sudden anxiety filled her chest. She grabbed her mother's hand. "Where…the kids?"

"Don't worry about them. They're at Missy Jenkins's." She continued smoothing Rachel's hair. "I didn't want them staying at my place until they find the intruder, and she already has one of my keys. She can pop in and grab more diapers or whatever she needs."

Releasing her panic on a long exhale, Rachel gave her mom a faint smile. With a new baby of her own, Missy was one of the few people, besides her mom, who she trusted to watch Brad and Daisy.

"Thirsty." Rachel tapped a finger against her throat.

"Oh my goodness. Where's my head?" Her mom pushed the call button, and when a nurse answered, she informed her Rachel was awake, asked for more ice chips and warned about the slippery floor.

Still hovering over Rachel when the nurse came in, her mom finally stepped back toward her chair. A maintenance man followed the nurse, mopped up the melting chips on the floor and disappeared again.

The nurse, whose name tag read Amanda, held a thermometer in front of Rachel's forehead. "How are you feeling this morning?"

"Sore. I have a killer headache, and my scalp hurts when I touch it." She tried to swallow. "And I'm really thirsty."

"Just let me get your temp first." When the thermometer beeped, Amanda recorded the reading, then helped Rachel hold the cup and shake a few pieces into her mouth. "The headache is common with an injury like yours. And there are several places on your body, besides your head, that are going to be tender for a while. I'm going to update your chart, and the doctor will be in shortly to answer your questions and explain your next steps. I'm sure he'll okay something for the pain, but usually it's just Tylenol for the first couple days." She checked machines and glucose drips, making notes on her electronic pad.

"I'm going to stay until the doctor comes. I want to hear what he says." Her mom sat on the edge of the recliner. "Then I'll run home to freshen up and check on the kids. Is there anything you want me to bring you when I come back?"

"I can't think of anything." Rachel sighed. "Unless I'm going to be stuck here longer than today. If I am, I'll need a phone charger. And maybe the book on my nightstand."

"You usually have a few there waiting to be read. Which one do you want?"

"*Scent Detection*. It's that romantic suspense about a K-9 academy in Idaho."

Amanda glanced at Rachel. "You'll need clothes and shoes for whenever you do go home." Her gaze moved to Martina. "She came in barefoot, and the sheriff's office took the clothes she was wearing. Said they wanted to check for possible transfer evidence."

After the nurse left, her mom moved back to the bed and took Rachel's hand. "What happened last night, sweetie? I heard you scream and saw someone running away from the garage."

Before she could answer, the door swung open and the doctor who'd examined her the previous night came in.

"Well, you're certainly looking better today." Dr. Mason walked to the head of the bed and examined Rachel's scalp wound. "How are you feeling?"

"Sore all over, but the worst is a headache."

"You had a concussion, but the scans didn't show any serious damage. Your headaches should fade within a week." The doctor examined her other scrapes and bruises. "The most important thing is for you to take it easy for a minimum of two to three days, possibly as long as two weeks." When Rachel opened her mouth to protest, he added, "The rest of your body may be able to function, but your brain needs time to recover."

Frustrated that she might be dealing with a high-caliber headache for a week, she asked, "Is there anything I can take for the pain?"

Dr. Mason gave her a sympathetic smile. "I'll have the nurse get you some acetaminophen today. If everything still looks good this afternoon, I'll send you home with a prescription for ibuprofen or naproxen. It'll be safe to take one of those starting tomorrow."

"She'll be able to come home today?" Her mom's voice vibrated with relief. "That's wonderful. The kids will be so happy."

The doctor patted Rachel's blanketed foot. "How old are your kids?"

Her mother answered for her. "Her son is almost five, and the baby will be one in a couple of months."

He still addressed Rachel. "Do you have anyone who can help out with your children while you're recuperating?"

"Me." Her mom continued to do the talking. "We all pretty much live together, and I watch them when she's at work."

"That's good." The doctor turned enough to address

both women. "You'll be getting instructions when you go home, but I don't want you bending over for any reason, especially to pick up your kids. You're likely to have some dizziness, and you could fall, hurting yourself as well as the little ones." He glanced at her mom. "Make sure she doesn't. Absolutely no exercising or exerting herself."

Her mother nodded with such enthusiasm, Rachel was surprised she didn't salute.

"No driving," the doctor continued, now writing on his clipboard. "I'll want to see her before I authorize her to go back to work, so you or someone else will need to chauffeur her."

"I will." Her mom looked at Rachel as she said to the doctor, "I'll tie her to the bed if I have to."

Nodding, the doctor added, "It's best for your headache if you rest your eyes. I'd advise against watching television, using your phone or computer, even reading a book. Keep the lights low in here, maybe even off. That should help. Same thing at home." He stepped toward the door. "Any other questions?"

"I don't think so." Rachel looked to her mom, who shook her head. "At least not yet."

"All right. I'll check in on you later today." He flipped down the light switch on the wall as he left.

Then her mother played with the pull strings and twist rod until the blinds completely blocked out the relentless Texas sun. Rachel started to complain but stopped when the darkness eased her headache.

"There." She turned back to Rachel. "Now, can you tell me who attacked you last night?"

"I don't know. And it hurts too much to think right now." She pushed the button that lowered the top half of the bed.

"All right. You get some rest." She kissed Rachel's cheek. "I'm going to run. I'll be back quick as I can."

"No need to rush, Mom. Hopefully I'll go back to sleep." She yawned. "Oh, since I'm getting out today, don't bother with the book or charger. Give the kids a kiss and my love."

Once her mother had left, Rachel closed her eyes against the pain pulsating behind them. Images from last night flashed through her mind like a macabre slideshow. She tried to grab hold of details about the person who'd put her in the hospital, but each time she narrowed her focus, he evaporated like a wisp of black smoke.

A WHILE LATER—Rachel had no sense of time as it passed—the air pressure in the room changed. The door hadn't made a sound, but it had been opened, then closed. Soft taps on the floor—not a nurse's shoes, maybe someone tiptoeing—coming closer. A long pause, so long that she almost opened her eyes.

But if it was Marge, Bree or another friend stopping by to check on her, she had neither the energy nor the desire to visit.

Then the unique yet familiar scent of a particular gun cleaning solvent drifted to her. She'd first smelled it in high school when she sat next to Adam in a class. Now, she pulled it in with a deep breath and as it filled her, her eyes fluttered open of their own volition. Adam stood inches from the bed, his eyes locked on hers.

"Sorry, I didn't mean to wake you." He set a Sweets and Treats bag next to her cup of ice on the tray table. "I figured Brad might like some of his favorite candy, considering everything that's going on around him lately."

Rachel raised her bed to a sitting position and looked inside the bag. "How did you know he loves these?"

"I overheard you telling someone in the Busy B." A sheepish grin kicked up one corner of his mouth. "I would have gotten him a variety, but I wasn't sure what else he likes."

Rachel hefted the bag. "I think I'll have to hide most of this and ration it out to him. I can tell you've never had to deal with a five-year-old on a sugar high." She started to laugh, then stopped and put her hands to the sides of her head.

Adam's grin slipped as her face contorted with pain. "Are you all right?"

"Other than a killer headache and some bumps and bruises, I'm fine." She lowered her hands and closed her eyes for a moment, fighting off another rush of vertigo.

By the time she opened them, Adam had moved even closer, deep vertical lines etched between his brows. She tried to smile, to convey she was indeed fine, but the concern brimming in his eyes made it obvious she wasn't fooling him.

She dropped her gaze to the other things he held. "Are you visiting more patients this morning?"

He looked down, his eyes widening as if surprised, and coughed out an awkward laugh. "This is for you."

He set the plant on her table. "You mentioned you liked potted rather than cut flowers, so..."

He'd remembered a passing comment she made about flowers. Tilting her head to one side with care, she finally managed a real smile. "Daisies. You're good at figuring out people's favorites, aren't you?"

"Not usually. But I knew you'd named your daughter after your favorite, so it was easy to figure out."

He must have found that out the same way he discovered Brad's number one candy.

"Thank you, Adam. You didn't need to bring me anything."

He shrugged one shoulder, then set a box from the sweets store next to the daisies.

She picked it up and opened it. "Truffles. *Chocolate* truffles. Now, there's no way you could've figured this one out."

Her go-to treat to console herself on bad days or celebrate good ones was a chocolate truffle. Most of those occasions had been bad days during her marriage. And as Eric's ridicule of her pregnancy weight with Daisy had grown, especially after he saw her eating a chocolate, she'd taken to buying just one at a time and hiding it from him. She still considered them her secret guilty pleasure, even after kicking Eric to the curb. *And* having no plans to ever be pregnant again.

Been there, done that, got the stretch marks to prove it.

Rubbing the back of his neck, he looked down. "I may have gotten a hint from Sandy on those."

Thoughtful *and* honest.

Wonder why he hasn't been snatched up and married off by now.

"Oh, this is for Brad, too." He set a stuffed teddy bear next to the candy and plant. "And this one's for Daisy. It doesn't have any buttons or anything that she can eat or stick up her nose." He added a smaller bear, dressed in pink, to the overloaded table.

The larger bear was dressed in a baseball uniform, with a plush mitt covering his left hand and a plush ball sewn onto his right.

"They're adorable."

"I don't know if Brad's into baseball or anything, but I saw it at Frannie's and couldn't resist. Figured between Eric's…uh, and you getting hurt, it might take his mind off things a little."

"His favorite stuffed animal was his teddy, but we can't find it anywhere. I thought I'd collected all the kids' stuff from Eric's, but it must still be there."

"Yeah, um, there was a bear in his apartment." Adam shifted, as if uncomfortable. "You're not going to want it back."

She sobered for a moment, then pushed sad thoughts of Eric's death away. Smiling up at Adam, she said, "Thank you. He's going to love it. And this—" she picked up the smaller bear "—Daisy loves anything pink."

Adam nodded but didn't reply. His eyes narrowed as if assessing her stamina, then he pulled out his notepad and lowered himself into the visitor's chair.

"If you're feeling up to it, I need to ask you a few questions about last night."

"Sure." Rachel grabbed her cup of ice and tapped a few pieces into her mouth.

"Why don't you just start from the beginning and tell me what happened?" He rested his ankle across the opposite knee.

After walking Adam through the previous evening she'd spent with her mom, she gulped another few chips of ice. "I was exhausted. From finding out Eric was dead to dealing with Dave at your office, yesterday was not a good day. Mom suggested I go relax, so I headed up the outside garage stairs to my apartment."

"Did anything seem different? A dark window when you'd left a light on, or vice versa? Did you sense anything?"

"No." She paused. Her answer had been automatic. She closed her eyes and revisited every step, every sound she might have ignored. "I heard a noise. But I didn't hear it again, so I thought it was probably nothing. When I opened the door, it was dark inside. I'd left a light on, and I figured the bulb had burned out." She opened her eyes. "When I pushed my door open, a black blur came at me. Knocked me backward and down the stairs. And that's the last thing I remember." Frustration at losing even a short period of time ate at her.

"Do you remember unlocking your door before opening it?"

"It wasn't locked. I never lock the door when the kids and I are just downstairs at Mom's." At his admonishing look, she shrugged a sore shoulder. "There's never been a need."

"So whoever was in there wouldn't have had to pick the lock or force his way inside." Adam tapped his pen against his notepad. "Can you close your eyes again and picture the moment he ran into you? Exactly what did you see? What did you feel? Did you hear anything?"

Rachel did as Adam asked, letting her mind drift on its own instead of forcing it. "I turned the knob and pushed the door open, but not quite all the way. It was dark inside." She frowned. "I reached along the wall for the light switch, but before my fingers touched it, something even darker than the apartment came at me." She still couldn't get a firm grasp on her assailant's appearance. "A person. His head was too big and he… he had no face. He pushed me, and I grabbed his arm out of reflex. You know, trying to stop myself from going backward."

Rachel's breaths accelerated, and in the background the EKG machine beeped faster. "He wore something soft, maybe a sweatshirt. He yanked it from my grasp… When his hand slid through mine, it was soft. Like skin, but with texture. Maybe a glove." Her eyes popped open in surprise. "I think he was wearing a ski mask. There was a quick glint, about where his eyes would be, but it was more like an impression."

"Your mom saw someone run down the driveway and around the front of her house, but she thought he was wearing a hoodie. Maybe that accounted for his head being too big."

"You've talked to Mom already?"

Standing, Adam nodded. “We had plenty of time to chat last night before the doctors were done with you.”

“Last night? I thought I just dreamed you were here.” Rachel’s cheeks warmed at the implication, and she dropped her gaze to her lap.

He chuckled. “You may have, because you were sound asleep. I stayed while Martina went home to get some things, then left when she got back.”

A rush of fear passed through her. “This has something to do with Eric’s murder, doesn’t it? I mean, it’s too much of a coincidence, all this happening at the same time.” She grabbed his hand. “What about my kids? My mom? If I’m in danger, aren’t they?”

“For now, we need to assume the two things are connected. Your mom will be back up here today, right?” When Rachel nodded, he continued. “I can have a deputy swing by your neighbor’s place throughout the day and check on your kids. Do you know how long you’ll be in the hospital?”

“They’ll most likely discharge me late this afternoon or early evening. But there’s no way we can stay at my mom’s. What if he comes back? I can’t—” Even to her own ears, she was spiraling, and it wasn’t like her. Her voice climbing higher, her words coming faster, her head about to explode from her rising panic.

Adam clasped both her hands. “Rachel, calm down. I’ll figure out somewhere else for you and your family to stay.”

After taking a deep breath, then exhaling, Rachel spoke in a more normal tone. “Don’t tell me to calm down.” Her maternal extinct overrode her filter. “You don't have kids, so you couldn't possibly understand that a parent will *die* to protect their children. A parent will kill to protect them, too."

Chapter Seven

Twenty minutes after he left the hospital, Adam was in his office, focused on work. Checking the department schedule, he noted Sean and Pete had the weekend off. He made some notes to rearrange cases and patrols on Monday, freeing himself up to concentrate on the Miller cases.

He brought up his phone's speed-dial list and tapped one.

"I'm not coming in today, and you can't make me." Pete's droll greeting made Adam laugh.

"I don't need you to come in. But I'm curious if you're busy today."

"Just enjoying my time off." Pete's ability to keep his entire existence a mystery continued.

"You live up on the north side of town, don't you?"

"Depends. What do you want?"

"I need someone to do protective drive-bys of the Novotny property at 2249 Elm. No need to sit on it all day, just pass by every hour."

"Yeah, I'm not too far from there. Once an hour enough?"

"Should be. You hear about the break-in there last night?"

"No. When it's my day off, I make a practice of *not* listening to police calls."

"Got it." Adam didn't blame him. "The garage apartment was broken into. Rachel Miller was hurt. I want to make sure no one breaks into the main house."

"From the Busy B?" Pete's seriousness kicked in. "She okay?"

A mental image of Rachel's injuries caused a sudden chill that made goose bumps along his arms. "She'll live. Listen, Pete, watch the house next door, too. Missy Jenkins. She's got Rachel's kids there with her today."

"I think half-hour passes are more in order, considering the children. I'm on my way." The phone went dead.

Pete's priorities sure popped into place with the mention of kids. Interesting.

Next, he called Bree. "You here in the building?"

"Five minutes away." She cursed at a driver. "I'll come straight to your office."

While he waited, Adam mulled over his earlier conversation with Rachel. Her sudden panic attack in the hospital had surprised him. Not that she shouldn't be worried about her family. But in all the years he'd known her, even in her worst moments she always remained calm and in control. Attributing it to side effects from her concussion, he brushed off her harsh remarks about him not understanding. Because he did, even if he didn't have kids. Yet.

After a single knock on his door, Bree came in without waiting for an invitation. "Sorry, Adam." She sat in one of the two visitor's chairs, pushing her braid back over her shoulder.

"No excuse for why you weren't here, waiting for me?" His stern tone hid his amusement at her frazzled entry.

Straightening her back, Bree folded her hands on top of Adam's desk and cleared her throat. "If you'd like a *reason*, I'm happy to give you one." She waited him out for a moment. "You."

"Me?" He leaned back in his chair and stretched out his legs. "I can't wait to hear this."

"You assigned Noah to patrol to the north."

"I did." Resting his elbows on the chair arms, he tented his forefingers and rested them against his bottom lip. "And when he and Dave are finished, they'll patrol the south part of the county."

Bree rolled her eyes, then settled them in a glare aimed at Adam. "He'd planned to have breakfast with Nate."

"I know that."

"So you sent your brother out on the one task he hates more than any other, while cantankerous, hungry and in need of his extra-extra coffee."

"I'm assuming you, being the sweet, loving fiancée that you are, decided to take him his sorely missed food and coffee."

"Darn tootin' I took it to him. I'm the one who has to live with him." She unfolded her hands and relaxed against the back of her chair. "When you told me I'm working the Miller cases with you, I thought you said you had some assignment in mind for him. And don't you dare tell me it's just patrolling the boonies."

Adam couldn't help but laugh. "That *would* make his life miserable, wouldn't it?"

"His? It would make *my* life unbearable." Her brows pulled into an upside-down V. "I'm not discussing murders or break-ins until you tell me what it is."

"I think Noah's having a bad influence on you." He narrowed his eyes. "You do remember I'm your boss, right?"

Chastised, Bree let her head fall forward and looked down at her lap. "Sorry, Chief Deputy Reed. Sir." When she raised her eyes just enough to meet his, a mischievous grin danced on her lips.

"Yep, definitely spending too much time with Noah." He chuckled. "And it's not patrol."

With a single nod of acknowledgment, Bree turned on her department tablet. "First, on the break-in, I didn't find *much* inside the apartment. I printed the light switch and doorknob, but—"

"Rachel said the perp was wearing gloves." Adam tapped his computer, waking it up.

Bree made a note of that. "I think he was looking for something specific. Everything that could be was slashed, including her mattress. Dresser drawers were dumped upside down, everything in them strewn across the floor. Even the kids' room had been tossed." Bree glanced at Adam. "There's something particularly disgusting about a slashed crib mattress."

Adam pushed away the disturbing image. "Which means it must be something relatively small." He scanned the digital report Bree had started. "Do you know if she has any expensive jewelry? A ring, anything?"

"I've never noticed her wearing any jewelry, but it's possible."

"You texted last night you thought you might've found something."

Bree opened her phone and pulled up a picture. "Not too far inside the front door, I found this under a pillow." She handed him her phone.

"A blank piece of paper?" He enlarged the picture as much as possible without it pixelating. "Why would this be interesting?"

"I'm not sure it is. But it struck me as out of place. Long, narrow piece of paper, ripped in one place." She reached out for her phone. "I didn't see anything else like it in her apartment. And as I was leaving, I found this outside, up against the side of Martina's house."

Adam took her phone again and examined the next picture. A paper just like the first one. But this one lay partially on grass, the rest of it held against the house's foundation by last night's breeze.

"I collected them and entered them both into evidence. But I don't know if they're important." Bree closed her phone and left it on Adam's desk.

Frustrated with the little they had to go on, he opened another report. "All right, let's set the break-in aside and look at Eric's murder."

When Bree got the report open on her tablet, her eyes widened. "That's a lot of blood."

"Several stab wounds to the chest and slashed carotid." Adam scrolled through more photos. "When the forensics team rolled him on his side, they found more wounds on his upper back."

Bree rolled her lips between her teeth. Adam had noticed she did that when she wanted to stop herself from saying something.

"What?"

"I hate to even think this, but that many stab wounds..." Her upbeat demeanor disappeared.

"Looks like a crime of passion?" Adam finished her thought. "Unfortunately, it does."

"There's no way Rachel would've done this." Bree's braid swung with each shake of her head. "No way."

"We have to look into every possibility. You know that."

"Maybe he got another woman mad enough at him to do this." She motioned toward the pictures. "Or he could have been seeing a married woman, and the husband came after him."

"Again, we'll look into everyone. We need to do a full background check on Eric. His phone was locked with a password, so we're waiting for the call records from his carrier. In the meantime, forensics is trying to get into it. He might have pictures that would help." He paused while Bree caught up to him with her notes. "Check social media, see if he had any accounts. I know he frequented the Dead End. I need to talk to the bartender, see if he hung out with anyone in particular there."

"Or if he came in with, or met, a particular woman

there." Bree tapped her pen. "Do you know where he worked?"

"Only that he did construction and manual-labor jobs that paid under the table. At least, according to Marge." Although some put no stock in the gossip shared by the owner of the Busy B, Adam often found her as useful as a confidential informant. "I'm going back to both scenes this afternoon. Why don't you start the background on him. And plan on working tomorrow, okay? I want to stay on this."

"No problem." Bree leaned her elbow on the desk and propped her chin in her palm, scrolling through both crime scenes' photos. "It's obvious the perp was looking for something. I just can't figure out why he would think Rachel had it. Or how he even found Rachel."

"Maybe Eric told him he gave whatever it is to Rachel." Adam's stomach churned at the possibility. A man had to be lower than a snake in a wagon rut to put a woman in danger. "And we need to find the stranger Eric fought with Friday night at the bar. My gut tells me he's somehow involved in all this, and I got a good enough look at his face to recognize him if I see him again."

Reading from her tablet, Bree ran through her notes. "To recap, Eric and a stranger fought at the Dead End Friday night. Eric spent the weekend in jail. He and Rachel had an argument early Monday afternoon. Eric was killed sometime between Monday afternoon and Friday morning, and Friday night Rachel's apartment was broken into and she was shoved down the stairs."

Adam stood, signaling the meeting was drawing to a close.

"I understand we have to consider Rachel a suspect in Eric's death." Bree closed her tablet and rose. "But wouldn't the fact that someone attacked her be proof of her innocence?"

"Hopefully. But her last words to Eric during their argument were if he came near her kids again, it would be the last thing he ever did."

Bree muttered a curse under her breath.

"Call me if you find anything important in his background or social-media stuff. I'm heading over to the Dead End." Adam followed her out of his office, pulling his door shut behind him.

Settling his Stetson on his head, he strode to his SUV, with some other words of Rachel's echoing in his mind.

A parent will die to protect their children. A parent will kill to protect them, too.

"BECAUSE IT'S THE best idea, Mom." Rachel leaned back against her raised bed, glad the Tylenol was helping with her headache. "If you and the kids are at Aunt Sylvie's in San Antonio, I'll know you're safe and I won't have to worry about you."

"It's ridiculous. You know Sylvie doesn't like children. She's not going to let us stay with her." Martina plopped down on the visitor's chair.

"Even if your lives are in danger?" Rachel had no siblings, but she couldn't imagine her aunt refusing to help her own sister.

Martina tapped a finger against her lips. She pulled her phone from a tote bag big enough to use as a suitcase. "But I still don't want to leave you here by yourself."

"Mother." Calling her mom by this instead of just *Mom* was the equivalent of a parent using a child's middle name. "I'm asking you to keep my children, your grandchildren, safe."

"I'll do it under one condition. You come with us." Martina leaned forward and reached for Rachel's hand. "You can recuperate in San Antonio instead of here."

Instead of arguing the point, Rachel said, "Call Aunt Sylvie. See what she says."

While her mother was on the phone, Rachel checked her own for messages. Marge had left a feel-better-soon voice mail, and she had a recent text.

Adam: Just checking in. How are you feeling?

Rachel: Better. Getting out soon.

Adam: Where r u going?

Rachel: Begging Mom to take kids to SA.

Adam: And you?

Rachel texted the shrug emoji and closed her phone as her mom ended her call.

"We can stay with Sylvie," Martina announced with a triumphant attitude. "She's not thrilled about the kids, but she'll fall in love with them once we're there. And she said she has some fancy shindig to go to this evening, but she always keeps a spare key in one of those fake rocks near the back door."

Not necessarily a safe idea, but, oh well. "Thanks, Mom. I appreciate you doing this."

"I better get home and pack us all bags, grab the kids and their stuff." Martina stood. "I'll be back to pick you up."

"Sounds perfect. I'll be ready to go as soon as they release me." She hated to lie to her mom, even by omission. But the top priority now was to get them to safety. "But I'm pretty sure my apartment's still a crime scene, so I don't think you can go in there for my clothes."

"Oh dear." A frown crossed her mom's face before she brightened. "I washed that basket of laundry you brought over yesterday morning. I'll pack that, and we can pick up anything else you need after we get to Sylvie's."

After her mother left, Rachel grabbed her phone and called the diner.

"Busy B Café." Marge's rushed greeting was followed by her hand over the receiver while she yelled at the cook to hurry up with the orders. "Sorry about that. I'm shorthanded today. Did you want to place a pickup order?"

"It's Rachel."

"Rachel, sweetie, how are you? I left a message for you earlier, you were probably sleeping. Is everything okay? I'll be up to visit you tomorrow before I open."

"I'm fine, thanks. I did get your message." Rachel took a sip of water. "Here's the thing. I'm getting out today, and I need to find a place to stay. I don't feel safe going back to Mom's house or my apartment until they find whoever broke in."

"Say no more, sweetie. I'll call Doc, tell him to set you up with the best room he's got. Or do you want two? You need a crib and a cot for the little ones?"

"Marge, you're a lifesaver. One room is fine. Mom is taking the kids to her sister's in San Antonio." She wiped a damp eye, blaming her emotions on the concussion. "I can't thank you enough."

"No thanks needed. Happy to do it, and Doc will be, too." She covered the receiver and hollered again. "Gotta go, hon. We got a late lunch-hour crowd."

Rachel stared at her phone for a minute, then texted Adam.

Need ride this afternoon.

ADAM REMOVED HIS sunglasses and let his eyes adjust to the dark interior of the Dead End. The midafternoon crowd was sparse, even with it being Saturday. The noise level was low, other than a few hard-core drinkers at the bar, two bikers playing pool and an Astros spring-training game on the suspended flat-screens.

"Hey, Adam. Draft or bottle?" Behind the bar, Max sliced limes in preparation for the busy night ahead.

"Can't, on duty." Adam tipped his head toward the far end of the bar, where no one sat. He took the last stool and waited for Max to join him.

Max wiped a towel across the already-dry bar top. "What's up?"

"That fight a week ago, Eric Miller and that stranger. You know what started it?" Adam took a stir stick from the container and stuck it between his teeth.

"First off, I'm not so sure the other guy *was* a stranger. Least, not to Eric." Max leaned his elbows on the bar and kept his voice low. "The other guy came in first, sat at that far table—" he nodded to a corner four-top "—with his back to the wall. Eric came in five, maybe ten minutes later, walked straight over and sat across from him."

"Did they start arguing right away?"

Max shrugged, his thick neck sinking into his shoulders. "It was busy, so I wasn't focused on them. But I never did see the other guy smile. And Eric seemed nervous from the get-go."

"You see Eric in here with a lot of different women? Or one in particular?"

"He never came in with one. After a couple drinks, he'd start schmoozing with the ones who weren't already with a guy." Max turned at the sound of his name. "Hang on a sec."

While Max returned to the taps to fill another pitcher for the bikers, Adam spun his stool around and surveyed the entire space. He'd come here a few times after he first got home from college, it being one of Resolute's few nightlife opportunities. But the dance between drunk cowboys wanting a night of pleasure and lonely women needing proof of their appeal just made him sad. Nothing he wanted in life would ever be found in the Dead End.

When Max returned, Adam asked, "Did you hear anything they said, anything that led to the fight?"

"Not really. Eric kept his voice low the whole time. The other guy asked him where something was. But I was busy with the crowd, and next thing I know they're destroying my bar." Max waved at someone coming through the door.

"Thanks." Adam gave in to his curiosity and, as he stood, asked one more question. "You remember how far back it was when Eric started coming in here, schmoozing with the women?"

"For years, man. A lot of years."

Adam nodded, his mouth in a tight line. No surprise there.

Chapter Eight

Adam paused outside Rachel's hospital room, smiling at the scene through the open door.

"Mom, I can't leave yet." While Rachel balanced Daisy on her lap, Brad sat on the hospital bed next to her, playing with his new baseball bear. "They haven't released me, and I don't want you to wait around and then drive to Aunt Sylvie's after dark. Besides, Dr. Mason wants to see me in a few days for a follow-up."

"They have doctors in San Antonio that can check on you in a few days." Martina crossed her arms over her chest.

"I only want to deal with one doctor. As soon as he clears me, I'll be right behind you." Both of their voices rose with emotion.

Adam eased into the room with a hesitant smile. "Is it safe to come in?"

"Adam." Martina held her hands out toward him. "Please talk some sense into my stubborn daughter. It's not safe for her to stay here. She needs to leave town with the kids and me."

"Adam, will you please tell my headstrong mother

that I'll be perfectly safe here?" Rachel signaled him behind her mother's back to agree with her.

"I understand your concern, Martina." Jumping into the middle of a mother-daughter argument was a no-win situation for him. "And I hate to bring this up right now, but Rachel needs to stay in Resolute." He glanced at the kids, not wanting to say anything that might upset them. "Because of the, um, ongoing investigation we started yesterday."

Martina's mouth dropped open. "Are you serious? You're still considering her a suspect?" She threw her hands up in the air. "Well, she certainly can't go home. Where's she going to stay?" Even the kids glanced up at this high-pitched outburst from their meemaw.

Trying to keep the kids calm, Adam summoned a mellow tone. "I'll find somewhere safe for her to stay."

Martina spun back toward the bed, glaring at her daughter. "You lied to me. You said you'd come with us."

"I didn't lie, Mom." Rachel handed Daisy the small pink bear, avoiding her mother's eyes. "I just remembered about the follow-up visit while you were gone. And Adam never told me I had to stay in town."

When her gaze met Adam's, her cheeks reddened before she could look away. *Good to know she blushes when she lies.*

"Well, I guess we should get going, then." Martina straightened her back and picked up her tote bag. "Give your mommy a kiss, Brad." She rounded the bed to take Daisy.

Still holding on to the baby, Rachel hugged Brad

to her. "Honey, Deputy Reed is the one who brought you your bear and your favorite candy. What do you say to him?"

The little boy looked at Adam, then buried his face against Rachel's side.

"Can you thank him, Brad?" Rachel kissed Daisy and handed her to Martina.

Holding the bear out toward Adam with one hand, Brad peeked at him and mumbled, "Thank you."

Brad crawled onto Rachel's lap as soon as Daisy had vacated the coveted spot.

"Mom, ration that candy, all right?" Rachel hugged her son. "You be a good boy and listen to Meemaw, okay?"

Nodding his head, Brad kicked at the bed rail that blocked him from climbing down. Adam leaned over and lifted him, holding him for a minute before setting him on the floor.

He wanted a houseful of little Brads and Daisys someday.

"Mom, call me when you get there, please?"

"Maybe I will, maybe I won't. I should let *you* see what it feels like to worry about your family." Martina doubled back from the door and kissed Rachel's forehead.

"Real mature, Mom."

Giving Adam a disappointed glare, Martina pushed Daisy's stroller with one hand, the other holding Brad's in a firm grip, and marched down the hall.

Adam cocked one brow at Rachel. "I have a feeling you didn't forget about the follow-up visit at all."

"I said whatever was necessary to get them to safety. By the way, thanks for the quick thinking, coming up with that don't leave town bit." When he didn't reply, she crossed her arms and scowled at him. "Are you telling me I really can't leave town? That I *am* a suspect?"

"I'm just following department procedures." He shrugged.

"You could have made that clear when you questioned me."

"I figured it was a moot point. I didn't think you'd have any reason to leave."

"And I still don't." She tried to see around him to the hall. "Are they gone yet?"

Adam looked past the nurses' station. "They're waiting for the elevator."

Rachel tossed the blanket to the side, revealing jean-clad legs. After pulling the cloth ties at the back of her neck loose, she yanked off her hospital johnny. Beneath it she wore a pale blue T-shirt that hadn't shown through the gown.

"Can you please help me get this bed rail down?" She grabbed hold of it but couldn't make it budge. "The nurse left it down earlier, but the first thing Mom did when she walked in was put both sides back up."

Adam held the rail where it was. "Why are you already dressed if they haven't even discharged you yet?"

She rolled her eyes, then closed them and shook her head in one smooth move. "As I said, I had to convince Mom to take the kids and get the heck out of Dodge." They had a momentary staring contest until she rattled the rail. "Well?"

Adam unlocked the rail and moved it down. "I admire your intent, but your ability to lie concerns me."

Pushing the call button, she didn't respond. When a nurse answered, Rachel said, "I'm ready to leave now."

"I'll send the orderly in," the disembodied voice replied.

Pushing her feet into a pair of tied sneakers, Rachel glanced up at Adam. "I'm really not good at lying, and I hate to do it. But for the sake of Mom and my kids, I had to stretch the truth a little."

"Why *were* you so adamant about staying in Resolute before you even knew you have to stay?"

"I have a job. Between the cut on my hand and this, I've already left Marge shorthanded for three days. She needs me, and I need the job. Even though I pay the premiums, my health insurance is through the diner. And I've still got a big balance to pay on my college tuition."

"I thought you were just taking classes online."

"It's an online college. Less expensive than in person, but still not cheap." She dropped the box of truffles into a tote bag similar to her mom's and picked up her plant as an orderly pushed a wheelchair into the room. "But I'll graduate in a few months with a business degree. I've already had job offers as an administrative assistant from companies in Houston and Dallas."

At a loss for words, Adam picked up her small suitcase and brought up the tail end of the convoy. Rachel chatted with the orderly as he wheeled her to the elevator, oblivious to the fact she'd just crushed the tiny bit of hope Adam had hidden away.

Elbow on the center console of Adam's truck, Rachel propped her forehead against her fingers. The headache had returned, and it was raging. Parked in front of the last in a row of detached rooms at Doc's Motor Court, she closed her eyes and took a deep breath.

"You overdid it, didn't you?" At Adam's voice, soft and nonjudgmental, she raised her head. "I can see the pain in your eyes. Stay here. I'll go get the key from Doc."

He'd been put out with her for not being honest with her mom, but he hadn't said a word since they'd left the hospital parking lot. Her head had appreciated the silence, even if instinct told her he wasn't happy.

When he returned, Adam propped open the door to her room, then helped her out of the truck. "I figured my own vehicle would draw less attention, but I didn't think about the step."

"At least you've got a running board. It's not hard." Just as the last word left her mouth, her shoe slid off the edge and she fell forward into Adam's arms. "I've always been a bit clumsy."

"You were never clumsy. This is the concussion and the long day catching up with you." He held her until her feet were firmly beneath her. "It's been less than twenty-four hours since your noggin got conked."

She giggled. "I did conk my noggin pretty hard."

"Let's just get you inside, okay?" He lifted her bridal-style, carried her through the doorway and set her on the bed. "I'll get your stuff."

Rachel didn't argue.

He managed it all in one trip, and after he closed the

door, he set the daisies on the bedside table. "Are your prescriptions in the suitcase or tote bag?"

Rachel palmed her forehead and fell back against her pillows. "They're at the pharmacy. I forgot about them."

"No problem. I'll pick them up." He walked into the kitchenette and opened, then closed, the refrigerator. "You'll need groceries, too."

"I'll get them later." Her head hurt too much to think about food.

"Tell me what you want."

She lifted her head. Adam, sitting in a chair near the bed, held a small notebook and a pen. She rolled her eyes and dropped back onto the pillows.

"Better tell me, or I'll be coming back with rib eyes and whiskey."

"I don't think I'm quite ready for that yet." Looking up at the ceiling, she rattled off a short list of foods, including her favorite cookies. She already missed her kids. And now she was without her mom, her rock, always there for her during her darkest days. She'd definitely need cookies this week.

His voice closer to her now, Adam asked, "Anything else?"

"No." Her eyes moved to the right and found Adam looking down at her. She smiled. "Thank you. For everything."

He saw her smile and raised her a wink. "Don't move until I get back." And with that, he was gone.

Rachel rotated her head and eyed her pot of flowers. She'd kept one arm curled around them the entire drive from the hospital. Adam certainly seemed to run hot and cold. He'd seemed angry earlier, but now he was bending over backward with kindness. She stretched out her arm and touched a flower with her finger.

Daisies never tell, do they?

Her eyes drifted closed, and in her dream, she slept alone in a field of giant daisies, all whispering, *He loves you...he loves you not.* Over and over and…

LATE MONDAY MORNING Adam glanced up when Bree rapped on his open office door. He waved her in.

"I've got more information on Eric Miller." She settled into a chair and set a file folder on his desk. "I requested some of this Saturday, but apparently a lot of bureaucracy takes Sundays off. Go figure." Her mouth twitched, fighting a smile.

"Good thing we don't believe in all that red tape around here."

She opened the file folder. "Anyway, want to know what I found out?"

Adam nodded.

"Eric's prison records." Bree tapped the top paper. "Arrested at seventeen, tried as an adult and sentenced at eighteen on felony charges of burglary and aggravated assault. Sentenced to five years, out in two for good behavior plus time served awaiting trial."

Adam blew out a long, low whistle. "I wonder if Rachel knew about that when she married him."

"I don't know. But some women put up with a lot of stuff when they're in love." Bree flipped through papers in her folder, grabbed one and set it on top. "As far as social media, Eric didn't have accounts on any of the popular platforms. But…" She looked at him expectantly.

"Yes?"

"He had a Finder account."

"A dating app?" Adam shrugged. "He *is* divorced."

"Finder is more for hookups than finding forever love. But that's not the interesting part. Forensics were able to access his phone, and he downloaded the app as soon as he got out of prison." Bree frowned. "He was using it the entire time he was married to Rachel."

"We already knew he cheated on her. But seriously, how many matches could he have made in Resolute?"

"Other small towns, Victoria, even San Antonio, aren't out of the picture. It's possible someone else he was dating killed him." She muttered loud enough to be heard, "I probably would've."

"We can get the Finder info if we need it." Adam drummed his fingers on his desk. "But it did look like a crime of passion."

"Maybe one of his Finder swipe-rights was more passionate than he was."

He glanced up, met Bree's gaze, and they both looked away. Neither mentioned Rachel's name.

"This is good work. Despite having to consider all possibilities, I keep coming back to the guy Eric fought with at the Dead End. Like we agreed at Rachel's apartment, his death and her break-in seem too coincidental to ignore."

Bree nodded, then suddenly brightened. "Hey, I forgot to tell you. Cassie's attorney friend came through big-time for the youth program. You know that dollar store on Henderson that went belly-up about five years ago?"

"Yeah. The building's been sitting empty ever since."

"Well, this assistant DA, Sara Bennett, contacted the building's owner, and he's decided to donate the building to us. We won't have to pay rent, and he can deduct it as a charitable contribution." Her grin got even bigger. "Sara knows the county council is still dragging their heels on allocating part of their budget to the program, so she's giving us what we need to get the building ready to use, and a crew's already working on it. We're hoping for a ribbon cutting in a few months."

"That's great, rookie. I'm impressed by how fast you got the ball rolling on this thing."

As a kid getting into trouble in San Antonio, Bree had wound up in a youth program run by cops. When she became a cop herself, she initiated a similar program through her precinct in the same city. She brought her passion for helping kids stay out of detention centers and correctional institutions with her when she became a Boone County deputy. Seeing the need firsthand during a drug case she and Noah had worked back in January, she let Cassie know what she wanted to do. Between Bree, Cassie, Sara Bennett and a little extra pressure on the county council from Adam, the Boone County Youth Program was coming to fruition.

His cell phone rang, and he answered as soon as he saw Rachel's name on the screen. "Hi. Is anything wrong?"

"No, no. I hate to bother you, but I have my follow-up with the doctor this morning. They worked me in last minute, otherwise I would have arranged this sooner."

"I'm on my way."

Bree's forehead crinkled in concern. "What's wrong? Was that Rachel? Is she okay?"

"She's fine. She just needs a ride." Adam grabbed his hat and opened the door.

"I can take her. You've got more important things to do." She rose and followed him toward the lobby. "Adam, I'm happy to—"

"Keep working the case, Delgado." As he passed Helen's desk he said, "Be back in a while."

"Where are you going?" Helen called after him.

Adam didn't bother to answer. Bree would tell Helen, and then they'd discuss his insistence on driving Rachel himself and what deep meaning it held.

Usually that would bother him. But right now, all he cared about was that Rachel was doing well. Just one weekend between her fall and this follow-up didn't seem like enough time for her recovery. Unwilling to take any chances on a setback, Adam wanted to hear the doctor's opinion himself.

He was pretty sure Rachel wouldn't agree to that, but he had an idea about how to convince her.

Chapter Nine

“Isn’t this a little soon for your follow-up?” Adam waited until he’d parked in front of the medical building to ask, fearing a silent ride if Rachel got defensive. “I thought your doctor said it would be several days.”

She shrugged as she unbuckled her seat belt. “I’m feeling great, and he’s willing to see me today.” She turned her head toward him and smiled. “Thanks for this.”

And just like that, despite his concern that she was rushing things, his day got a little better.

He climbed out of his cruiser and met her in front of it.

Rachel crossed her arms over her chest. “What are you doing?”

“Going inside with you.”

“Thanks, but you don’t need to do that.” Her polite words failed to gloss over her sharp tone.

“I know, but I’m sure I’ll be more comfortable waiting inside.” His reason for accompanying her left Rachel no room to argue.

She led the way inside and to the elevator. When

they found the correct office, she checked in at the desk while Adam took a seat in the small waiting area. Rachel had chatted during the ride from Doc's to the doctor's, but now she took the chair next to him and remained quiet.

"I'd like to go in with you, hear what the doctor says."

Rachel shifted in her chair, turning toward him. "Absolutely not. That's an invasion of my privacy."

"Not if you allow me to."

"What makes you think I would?" She scoffed. "It's none of your business."

"Hear me out, okay?" When she turned back, ready to argue, he held up a hand in front of him like a stop sign. She glared at him but remained silent, so he continued. "I know you're champing at the bit to get back to your normal routine. But if you're not quite ready, not only could you compromise your physical health, but you also might become vulnerable to someone who's after you."

"What you're really saying is that you don't believe I'll tell you the truth about what the doctor decides. The bottom line is you don't trust me." Her voice quivered with anger.

"I can't forget how you tricked your mom into taking the kids out of town without you." Adam shrugged. "I just want to make sure you don't overdo it too soon."

"I told Mom what I had to for her and the kids' safety. But I've never lied to you." She sighed. "Not even a single tiny fib."

"Look, Rachel, it's just—"

"Remember when I came to your office to be questioned?" When he nodded, Rachel went on. "You asked me to trust you that day. I didn't have to. I really had no good reason to. But I did. And now I'm asking *you* to trust *me*. Trust me to tell you the truth about the doctor's decision, good or bad."

Adam swallowed past a lump forming in his chest. A lump of self-reproach, of contempt for his seemingly self-righteous attitude. Rachel's point hit home, and it opened his eyes. Who was he to expect her to trust him, and then doubt her word? Caring about her was one thing. Demanding what amounted to a note from her doctor was something else entirely.

What compounded his sense of shame was his intended plan, a bargain not his to strike. If she allowed him to go in with her and the report was good, he'd take her to her place to get her car. How benevolent of him.

He raked his fingers through his hair. "I'm sorry. *Really* sorry. I do trust you."

Rachel gave him a sideways glance, as if waiting for his next ploy. But he didn't have one.

"I had no right to ask for, let alone expect, firsthand verification from your doctor. I let my concern for your well-being get out of hand." Raising his hand in a helpless gesture, he snorted at himself. "I've always been protective of my family, but I know them inside and out. I guess I didn't realize that when I try to protect someone who's not a Reed, I tend to get a bit overbearing."

Meeting his eyes, Rachel said, "A *bit*? And *overbearing* doesn't really say it all. You can be a domineering, presumptuous dictator who thinks everything's his way or the highway." She rested her hand on his forearm. "Look, I appreciate everything you've done and are doing. I'm grateful that you want to keep me safe. But you don't have to protect me from myself. I've got a family, too, and I'm not about to take unnecessary chances with my health. Okay?"

Adam nodded. "Got it."

"Good." Smiling, she patted his arm.

"Rachel Miller?" the woman at the desk called, as if the room was filled with patients. "The doctor will see you now."

As he watched Rachel follow the receptionist down the hall, he marveled at the intense sensation where she'd rested her hand on his arm. And he vowed he'd never ride roughshod over her sentiments again. Or at least, he'd try his best not to, no matter how hard it might be.

"SO, YOU'RE THE poster child for postconcussion recovery?" Adam drove north toward Rachel's apartment. "That's quite the compliment from a neurosurgeon."

"That's what the doctor said. I recovered faster than anyone expected. Faster than most of his other patients, even." Her smile was almost smug. "I can't wait to wash my hair tonight. I'm supposed to go back on Friday to get the staples out."

Glad that he'd come to his senses in the waiting room, Adam was enjoying Rachel's enthusiasm. She seemed to be back to her normal, high-spirited self, keeping the conversation going with little input from him.

"I do appreciate you taking me to my place. It's

weird how dependent I feel without my car." She drummed her fingers on her knees. "And I want to see how much of a mess I'll eventually have to clean up, whenever I get to move back in."

And that was the other reason Adam wanted to be with her today, or if it hadn't been today, whichever day she returned to her apartment for the first time. She expected a mess. What she wouldn't expect would be the emotional ambush waiting for her. The defilement of her personal space, her belongings. Her mom was out of town, and this wasn't anything she should go through by herself.

"When do you think you'll go back to work?"

"The doctor cleared me for everything, so I'll go by the diner when I leave here, see if Marge needs me today."

Regardless of the doctor's opinion, it seemed too soon for resuming full workdays. "Don't you think you should take it easy for a few more days, kind of ease back into work?"

"Adam, I feel fine. If I get tuckered out, I'll take a break. Or even go back to the motel early." Rachel nodded her head once, as if confirming this to herself. "I'm sure Marge will be lenient with my hours if I at least try to work."

"Probably so." He bit his lip to keep from disagreeing with her, before adding, "You're the best one to judge your endurance."

Her smile lit up her face. "I'm glad you see it that way."

Even if he didn't, he wasn't going to argue and upset

her again. Rachel was about to have more than enough to deal with the moment she stepped into her apartment. He was here to help her through that stressful situation, not cause her more aggravation.

He turned into her driveway and pulled all the way up to the garage.

"Thanks again for the ride. I, uh, guess you'll keep me updated on the case?"

"I'm going upstairs with you." Adam killed the engine and opened his door.

"I've already taken up enough of your time." Rachel scrambled out of the cruiser. "I'm just going to take a quick peek inside, grab a few things, and I'll be gone."

"Still coming with you." Adam followed her to the stairs, where she paused and looked down.

Taking in the still-reddish stain on the concrete landing, her face paled. "That's where I landed?"

"Yes." Adam stepped forward, took her arm and urged her up the first steps. "I'm coming with you because I want to make sure the perp didn't return. That he's not waiting inside for you." Only part of the reason, but she seemed more willing to accept physical protection than emotional support from him.

Rachel paused midstep. "You think that's possible?"

"Possible, but not very probable. Still, I'm not willing to take a chance. Are you?"

She shook her head and continued up to the door.

Adam took her keys and unlocked the door. "Let me just clear it before you come in. Okay?"

"Okay." She stepped back and held on to the top landing's railing.

It took Adam less than two minutes to make his way through the apartment, clear all the rooms and return. He held the door open for Rachel.

She took one step into the room and froze.

"You said it looked like someone had been searching for something." Rachel swiped away angry tears. "I didn't expect this level of vandalism." The furniture she'd scraped and saved for, cheap as it might be, ruined. Shelves toppled. Keepsakes broken.

"I know, it's a lot to take in." Adam put his arm around her shoulders. "But you won't have to clean everything up by yourself. We'll help you."

She stood, rooted to the same spot, one hand clasped over her mouth. How could she even have enough stuff to make this much of a mess? Her eyes traveled across the landfill that was her living room, lingering here and there. Pictures of Brad and Daisy tossed aside, the glass from the frames shattered. Books from her childhood that she'd kept for her kids, lying in awkward positions on the floor, their bindings broken and pages ripped out.

Looking toward the small galley kitchen to her left, she didn't trust her eyes. She stepped closer. Flour, sugar, spices, cereal, everything it seemed, formed a hill in the middle of the floor. Condiments were dumped on top of it. Milk cartons lay in the sink, empty.

She turned to face Adam. "I think I'd like to look at the rest of the rooms by myself."

"Are you sure? I—"

"I'm sure."

"Okay, I'll wait right outside. But holler if you need me for anything. Lifting something heavy, moral support, anything."

"I'm glad you insisted on staying." Rachel tried for a smile, but it was no use. "I just need some time alone to process this."

She closed the door behind Adam and took in the room one more time.

It's just stuff. It could've been worse.

The kids and I could be dead.

Even with the pep talk, she couldn't help but gasp at the sight of her kids' room. Brad's bed lay in pieces on the floor. Daisy's crib mattress had been slashed open, the foam inside yanked out. Picture books ripped apart, tiny clothes tossed about, toys broken. Even the piggy banks her mom had given each of the kids at birth had been smashed. The pink and blue porcelain shards littered the floor, surrounded by quarters. She seethed at the violation of her children's sanctuary.

She passed the bathroom without even a glance and stalled at the door to her room. The mess was no worse than the rest of the apartment. But tossed among the ripped pillows, slashed mattress, damaged books and shattered lamps was clothing from her dresser. She'd like to call it lingerie, but it wasn't. She'd quit buying anything close to lingerie after her first pregnancy. No, these were panties from the closest big-box store, sold in packages of five. Bras that came folded in boxes instead of hanging on cute little hangers.

She didn't care that her underclothes were cotton,

not silk. Utilitarian, not sexy. But the thought of some strange man touching them, even with gloved hands, turned her stomach. She'd come in here to grab more clothes, both outer and under. She left with nothing but the bitter taste of bile at the back of her throat.

Rachel stepped outside and locked the door behind her. Adam's forehead furrowed when he looked at her, so she assumed her face was broadcasting her thoughts, her feelings. She didn't care.

"You okay?" He was one riser behind her as she started down the stairs.

Her breath shaky, she managed, "Fine."

Halfway down, her nerves got the better of her and she reached for the handrail, but her fingers stopped just short of taking hold. The natural wood, worn by weather and darkened by years and years of hands, revealed its original light color beneath large missing splinters. Her hand went to one of the bandages on her opposite arm. Looking down at the steps ahead of her, she noticed another reddish stain on the edge of one. More blood. *Her* blood.

She'd taken control of her life the day she kicked Eric out. Since then, she had never backed away from a difficult situation. She wasn't about to start now, especially when the situation involved her kids' safety. When she reached the bottom landing, she straightened her spine and threw her shoulders back.

Nobody messes with my kids.

Adam's phone rang, and she waited while he took the call.

"Hi, Helen. What's up?" After listening a moment

he said, "No, I can take it. Text me the address, and have Noah meet me there." He pulled his cell away from his ear.

Noticing the tension in his voice, Rachel asked, "Something wrong?"

He hesitated for several seconds, as if not sure he should tell her. "Another dead body." He put his phone in his pocket and stepped closer to her. "If you're too upset to drive, I can take you back to Doc's on my way."

"Don't be ridiculous. I *am* upset, but I'm not going to let that creep take anything else from me, including a single minute more of my peace of mind. Once I'm busy at work, I won't even waste another thought on him."

"All right." He glanced at the garage. "I didn't clear it earlier. Is the door electric or manual?"

"Manual." Rachel unlocked it, and Adam motioned her to move off to the side.

Once she had moved, he opened the door and stepped inside, his hand on his gun. He looked in her car, poked at a tarp, then came back outside. "You're good to go."

"Thank you." This time she managed a smile for him, and he returned it.

"I'll touch base with you later. If you don't have any objections."

"I'd like that. And you can let me know if we've got a serial killer terrorizing Resolute or just a whole bunch of random thugs running amok."

"Deal." He left in a hurry, lights running but no siren.

Rachel backed her car onto the driveway. She closed and locked the garage and had one foot back in her car when Missy called to her.

"Whew! I guess I need to start working out again." Trying to catch her breath, she patted her postpregnancy tummy. "Are you all right? Your mom said y'all were going to San Antonio for a while."

"I'm good. Need to pace myself, but the doctor cleared me for normal activities." Rachel smiled, then flinched internally while Missy's eyes took in her bruises, partially shaved head and stitches. "It looks worse than it is."

"I'm sorry, I didn't mean to stare. I'm just surprised at your quick recovery." She glanced down, then seemed to surprise herself with something in her hand. "It's peculiar, but I found this in the opened canister of formula your mom gave me for Daisy." She held out her hand, a key lying on her palm.

Rachel took the key and examined it. "I've never seen this before."

"Well, I thought maybe it was to something important, so…" Missy shrugged.

Rachel didn't care if it was a key to Fort Knox, it shouldn't be in a formula can. After a quick mental inventory of Daisy's diaper bags, something clicked. "Maybe Mom gave you the bag I brought back from Eric's. There was a partial can in it when I gathered their stuff up." She nodded as if convincing herself. "It has to be his."

"I hope it's okay that I tossed the formula. Germs

and all." Missy scrunched up her nose and made a cute little *yuck* face.

"I'm glad you did. And, Missy, thanks. I really appreciate your help with the kids."

"Anytime." Missy gave a little *toodle-oo* wave with her fingers and jogged back toward her own house.

Rachel tossed the key in her purse and headed for town, chuckling at Missy's first-time-mom perfectionism. By the time her second kid came along, she'd hardly notice them eating dirt and keeping live bugs in their pockets.

RACHEL PARKED IN the rear alley fifteen minutes later and slipped into the Busy B through the kitchen door.

Marge marched over and took Rachel's hand in both of hers. "What in tarnation are you doing here? You're supposed to be recuperating." The older woman walked her over to the closest empty booth and made her sit. "You take it easy, and I'll bring you something to eat."

"I'm fine. The doctor cleared me. I'm here to work."

"You sure that doctor knows what he's doing?" Marge moved her forefinger in a circle in front of Rachel's nose. "Your eyes are squinting like your face hurts."

"Just a little headache. Nothing compared to the one I had Saturday." Rachel stood. "My uniform is at the motel. Luckily, Mom shoved it in a suitcase with my other clean laundry. But let me get my apron on. The lunch rush should start any minute now."

"You sure? I don't want you working before you're ready to."

"Thank you," Rachel said with a firm nod. "For everything. But I'm going crazy sitting around that motel room. I'm ready to work."

"Well, it's about time." Marge followed her into the back room. "I've been losing my mind since you wound up in the hospital, trying to do everything myself. Can't believe you're so clumsy as to fall down a whole flight of stairs." Her voice trembled on the last words.

Rachel spun around and wrapped Marge up in a strong hug. "I'm sorry I worried you."

Marge sniffled, then pushed Rachel away. "Hmph. I wasn't worried a bit. Everyone knows you've got a head hard enough to crack concrete, not the other way around." She turned her face to the side and swiped beneath her eyes.

"Well, then, I'm glad. I wouldn't want to upset an emotional wreck like you. You'd probably start crying and dropping to your knees in grief."

"Honey, if these old knees ever hit the ground, you'd have to call in the fire department to hoist me back up." Marge smiled. "Now get that apron on and get to work. Clock's a'tickin'."

A few regular customers welcomed her back with cheerful greetings and sympathy about her injuries. But as the afternoon wore on, the comments she overheard from other booths upset her.

A woman leaned across the table to address her husband in a low voice. "I always thought there was something off about her."

The manager of the grocery store confided to his three lunch companions in an overly loud whisper, "I never would have believed it, but I heard their argument. She threatened his life, and next thing you know he's dead."

"Maybe we should find another place for our weekly lunches," a middle-aged woman told her female friends. The other women nodded.

Exhausted by the time her shift ended, Rachel's head throbbed more than ever as she fought back tears and frustration. The same people she'd served for years with courtesy and respect, laughing at their jokes and responding to their chitchat, now believed she'd killed Eric. She'd thought Deputy Dave was a one-off. Just a bad-tempered cop hoping to pad his résumé by forcing her to confess. But after a day of almost no one meeting her eyes and receiving poor tips, it was obvious most of the rest of the town was of the same mind.

WHEN RACHEL TRUDGED to the front counter, Marge glanced at her. "You need shorter shifts if you insist on working this week." The older woman took her own apron off. "You look too beat to think straight. I'll drive you to the motel in your car. Doc can bring me back here."

"I appreciate the offer, but that's not necessary."

"It is if you want to keep this job. Now, go toss your apron in the laundry bin, and let's go."

Rachel did as she was told, then followed Marge through the kitchen and out the back door.

"Lee, I'm taking Rachel home. I'll be back in a few minutes."

The cook, sitting on a folding chair he kept in the alley for breaks, nodded.

"That means you stomp out that disgusting cigarette and get your skinny behind back inside. You need to watch the front until Cindy gets here."

Lee jumped to his feet and ground out his smoke beneath his shoe. "I didn't know she was workin' the dinner shift."

Cindy, the Busy B's part-time waitress, had captured Lee's heart on his first day at the diner. Unfortunately for him, his seemed to be a one-sided love.

"He better find someone else to get starry-eyed over, and soon," Marge grumbled, walking to Rachel's car. "I hate hiring new people, and I think Cindy's 'bout had enough of his crushing on her."

Rachel handed Marge the keys and walked to the passenger door. "They're about the same age, and sometimes there's no telling the heart."

Marge glared across the car's roof. "Then he needs to start talking louder to it."

Rachel laughed and climbed in after Marge popped the door locks.

On the drive to Doc's, Marge brought up the touchy subject of the customers. "I expect, from your mood by the end of your shift, that you heard people talking at lunch."

Rachel jerked her head toward her boss. "You've heard it, too?"

"It's been going on ever since word got out that Eric was dead. But you know how people who got nothing better to do like to gossip."

Rachel bit her tongue. Marge held the title of Gossip Queen in Resolute.

"Thing is," Marge continued, "it's nothing to worry about. I try to shut it down when I hear something, but it's all going to end as soon as Adam catches the real killer. You just need to ignore it in the meantime."

"That would be easier to do if they were talking behind my back. But they're intent on making sure I hear the ugly things they say."

"Rachel Miller, you know you didn't do it, so you just stand tall with your head held high."

Marge's resolute belief in her innocence did a lot to ease the hurt in her heart, but Rachel still needed more.

She needed to prove she didn't kill Eric.

COINCIDENCE HAD OFFICIALLY left the building. Adam looked down at the stranger who'd sucker punched him at the Dead End bar. The body of the man he suspected of killing Eric and hurting Rachel had been dumped along the side of a dirt road southeast of Resolute.

Shoving his hands into gloves he'd pulled from his pockets so he wouldn't contaminate the crime scene before the forensics team arrived, Adam marveled at the wounds inflicted on the deceased. Aside from a bruised and battered face, seven out of ten fingers had been cut off. One of the remaining was missing from the middle knuckle, another from the top joint. The nail had been pulled from the tenth one.

It seemed systematic, possibly ending when the killer learned what he'd been looking for.

Adam wore crime-scene booties as he worked his

way around the body, crouching for closer looks before moving on. The bottoms of the man's bare feet showed signs of burns. Not from a cigarette or a lighter—these wounds resembled those from electrical shocks. This on top of one missing ear, a sliced nose and lips that looked like amateur plastic surgery gone wrong.

And then the wound that most likely killed him, a jagged cut across the neck that stopped just short of the artery. The killer wanted the man to suffer right up to the end, choking on his own blood instead of a quick bleed-out. Distinctive markings along that cut piqued Adam's interest, as did the many odd-shaped, shallow puncture wounds on the body.

When Noah showed up, Adam directed him to string the tape in a wide circle around trees. They'd both approached the GPS location with care, stopping on the opposite side of the road a good way before the body in an effort to secure the killer's tire tracks.

"Damn!" Noah walked up to Adam after putting on his own gloves and booties. "He looks like a human dribble glass." Although improving, Noah still couldn't contain his irreverent sense of humor.

"This is the guy Eric Miller got in a fight with at the Dead End the Friday before he died."

"The one who punched you?" Noah chuckled. "Should I list you as a suspect? Person of interest due to a bruised face?"

"Curb the remarks before CSI gets here." Adam glanced at his watch. "Helen caught a team en route to another scene, and they're detouring here instead. Shouldn't be much longer."

"You think this guy killed Eric?" With a straight face now, Noah stepped where Adam had as he moved around the body, examining the extent of damage.

"I'm not sure what to think right now."

"At least Rachel's not a suspect. I mean, somebody coming after her proves that, right?" Noah's lips curled in disgust. "You see the scorch marks around his pants zipper?"

Adam had, but chose not to consider what they implied, his mind still preoccupied with the suspect list. "But does that automatically exclude Rachel? She fought with Eric, and he was found dead." He ticked off the points as he spoke. "Rachel's apartment is a mess, and she fell down her stairs. Does that automatically mean someone else did that to her? Or could she have trashed her own place and fallen down the stairs accidentally, or on purpose to look like a victim?"

Noah laughed, then sobered at the serious expression on his brother's face. "You can't possibly believe that."

Adam didn't want to. But want wasn't a factor. He needed to focus on facts. "The stranger Eric fought with is found dead after being tortured. What if Rachel, Eric and this guy were involved in something together? Maybe Rachel killed Eric, this guy attacked her and a new player killed this guy. Or maybe the new player was in on the whole thing with them."

"Bro, you're talking about Rachel. The girl you've wanted since the day you hit puberty."

"I have to consider every possibility. I can't blow

her off as a person of interest just because I liked her way back when." Adam massaged the back of his neck.

"Want to know what I think?" Noah finished circling the body and stopped next to Adam. "I think you're overcorrecting when it comes to Rachel. You're so afraid of showing her favoritism you're bending over backward to include her in the list of suspects."

Adam's jaw clenched at his little brother's perceptiveness, but he held his tongue.

"Rachel didn't kill this guy." Noah appraised the tortured murder victim with distaste. "Not unless she bought *The Complete Idiot's Guide to Torture* as well as *Torture for Dummies*." He snickered at his own poor joke.

At the sound of a vehicle, they both turned to look up the road. The forensics van pulled in behind their vehicles and parked.

"Hey, Adam. Noah." CSI Brett Miller and his team of techs and evidence handlers walked toward them, already wearing booties and gloves. "When I heard you had a body, I called dibs. Murders in Boone County are never boring for us."

Adam lifted his chin in greeting. Counties as small as Boone depended on the Austin crime lab for autopsies and evidence processing. Brett had been new to the lab less than a year ago, but now he was one of the best forensics investigators they had. When the CSI responded to Eric Miller's crime scene the previous week, Adam had been relieved to confirm Brett and the victim weren't related.

The team got to work while Adam kept a close eye

on their every move. After a few hours of setting markers by items and tracks, taking photographs and collecting evidence, a tech teased the deceased's wallet out of his pocket and opened it. He removed an expired Texas driver's license so Adam could take a picture of it.

Adam compared the license and picture to the body. "Richard Smith. Anything else in there of interest?"

"No credit cards. A picture of a brunette, almost too faded to make her out." The tech looked at the back of the photo. "No name." He dropped the wallet into an evidence bag, then searched the man's front pockets. Pulling out several items, he dropped them into another evidence bag, recording the contents as he worked. "Five quarters, two dimes, one poker chip, one torn piece of paper, one pair of nail clippers and one blue rabbit-foot key chain, no keys."

Brett joined Adam while the techs loaded the body into the van. "This guy made a very bad man very mad. You catch the signs of torture?"

Adam nodded. "Hard to miss."

"Think this is related to the other body we picked up last Friday?" Brett peeled off his gloves as the two walked toward the parked vehicles. "Or two completely separate cases?"

"Let's go with related for now. If y'all find anything in common between the two, let me know right away." Adam pulled off his booties and gloves, then opened his driver-side door. "And keep your fingers crossed no one else turns up dead around here."

"Now, that's taking all the fun out of my job." Brett slapped Adam on the back. "I'll be in touch."

Eager to get back to the office and figure out who Richard Smith had been, Adam made good time on the empty back roads to town. A block out from the justice center, his cell phone rang. Caller ID showed Marge's name.

"Hey, Marge. What's up?"

"You need to get over here to Doc's. It's about Rachel."

ADAM DROVE BENEATH the motel's retro stucco arch and parked in front of the office. Marge stood outside the glass door, waving at him, more frantic than he'd ever seen her.

"What happened? Is Rachel all right?" He reached for the door handle, but Marge stopped him.

"She's inside with Doc. She's upset, but she's okay." Marge, out of breath, inhaled. "She worked today, and I drove her home after her shift because she was tired. When she opened her room door, everything was all over the place. Clothes ripped and turned inside out, the mattress was catawampus, everything in her little fridge pulled out and dumped. The bathroom window had been broken out."

A powerful anger flowed through Adam. "Does Doc have security cameras?"

"Only for the front entrance and office. He looked at it. No one except customers drove in."

He yanked open the office door and held it for Marge before joining the small group inside. Marge's husband, Doc, sat next to Rachel on a small couch, one arm around her shoulders, his other hand holding hers. Several years older than his wife, he gave the impression of a kindly grandfather.

Adam crouched in front of Rachel. “Are you okay?”

“Yes.” The fear in her eyes said otherwise.

“Can you come with me to your room? Make sure I’m not missing anything?”

She nodded and slowly got to her feet.

“Doc, I need the security footage. How long before you record over it?”

“I keep it for a week. But I already went through today’s—”

“I’m not doubting you, but can you make me a copy of the past week’s, including today’s?”

Doc nodded. “You want it from both cameras?”

“Please.” Adam stopped Marge from following them as he opened the door for Rachel. “It’s a crime scene. Best if you wait here.”

“But I’ve already been in there, and—”

“Please, Marge. Just wait here.” Without waiting for a reply, he followed Rachel through the door.

“I can’t believe this is happening,” Rachel said as they crossed the parking lot. “Again. Today’s the first day I’ve even stepped out of the room. How did they find me?”

“I don’t know, yet. Think. What do you have that someone wants this badly?” Adam glanced at her, but she’d stopped moving.

“Are you serious?” Rachel planted her fists on her hips and stood her ground in the middle of the asphalt lot. "You think I knowingly have something that people are being killed for? And I'm willing to risk my life to keep it?" She turned away from him, her arms dropping to her sides, her hands still curled into fists.

"I had to ask, Rachel." He kept his voice soft, his tone soothing. "Whoever this is, they're not going to stop until they get what they want, or we catch them."

She spun back toward him. "Don't talk to me as if I'm a lunatic who needs to be calmed. I don't know who's looking for what. I don't know who killed Eric. I don't know who caused my concussion. And if you think I do, you're the one who's got a problem!" She was yelling by the time she finished, and a few motel guests had wandered out of their rooms to see what the excitement was about.

Adam reached to take her arm. "Let's finish this conversation in your room, okay?"

"No!" She jerked her arm away as if his touch burned. "If you honestly believe I'm responsible for any of this—" she waved her hands in the air "—I don't need your help. I don't *want* it."

In a low voice, Adam tried to reassure her. "That's not what I believe. And there's more that you don't know yet, but I'd rather talk about it where we won't be overheard."

He waited while she took several breaths to calm herself. When she began walking toward her room again, he fell in alongside her, staying silent. The swing-bar security lock had been flipped across to keep the door from closing tight. Adam pushed it open, held it for Rachel, then followed her in.

Adam stood just inside the entrance, surveying the entire room. This mess was different than the one in her apartment. Less chaotic. More intentional. And, somehow, more violent.

"I'm not accusing, just asking. Did Eric give you anything to keep for him? Probably something small, based on the searches. It could have been last week, last month, even longer ago."

She shook her head.

"What about the kids? Maybe a new toy that Brad brought home?"

Rachel scoffed. "Eric didn't even buy diapers for the baby. So no, no new toys."

"How well did you know Eric before you married him?"

"Well, obviously I misjudged his character, which is why I divorced him. And he lied. Cheated." Her voice grew softer as she spoke. "But other than that, I knew him as well as you can know anyone, I guess."

Adam took a deep breath. *No time like the present.* "Did you know that Eric spent time in prison?"

Rachel opened her mouth, closed it. "What are you talking about? Eric wasn't a model citizen, but he was never in prison."

Keeping a neutral expression, he held her gaze.

"You're serious, aren't you?" She sank onto the bed and gripped the edge of the mattress. "I can't believe…"

"I'm sorry you had to find out this way." He stopped short of pulling her to her feet and telling her to not touch anything. His gut told him there'd be no fingerprints in the room anyway, except those of guests and employees. Instead, he sat beside her.

"Why was he in prison?" Her question hung in the air like a half-deflated helium balloon.

"Burglary and aggravated assault. He served two years, got out shortly before he met you."

"If I'd known, I never would've gone out with him, let alone married him."

"I'm sure that's why he didn't tell you."

She ran a length of her long, dark blond hair through her fingers over and over, as if it soothed her. "I'm such a fool."

"Don't be so hard on yourself. How were you supposed to know? You trusted him, and he lied by omission. This is on him." Adam didn't want to make her go through another session of questions at the justice center, but Rachel might know something without even realizing it. He'd have to risk disclosing a few facts about the investigation in the hope of finding any random, unperceived clues from her. "Did Eric ever mention anyone named Richard Smith? Maybe as a friend or someone he worked with?"

Her brows pinched together in thought. "No. It's probably a common name, but I don't recall him mentioning it. I know we never had anyone by that name over when we were married. Why?"

"We think Smith is the person who killed Eric and broke into your apartment."

"And he's the one who followed me here? Broke in and trashed this room, too?"

"Whoever did this—" he motioned at the mess

"—isn't the same person who broke into your apartment."

"What makes you so sure? It looks the same."

"There are subtle differences. Richard Smith is the same man who fought with Eric at the Dead End. And he's dead. We found his body this afternoon."

Rachel closed her eyes as if she couldn't handle any more. "I'm confused. Eric said the other guy in the fight was a stranger."

"He told me the same thing."

Rachel's head swiveled toward him. "Was he killed the same way as Eric?"

"I can't discuss that with you." Adam took her hand. "But I think Eric got mixed up in something that was way over his head. I think that's what got him killed."

"First you thought I killed him. Now it's some invisible boogeyman." Her voice, cold and detached, chilled him. "You'll have to forgive me if I don't have confidence in your *thoughts*."

Her words cut him. She didn't understand the tightrope he'd been walking between his duties as a deputy and his belief in her innocence. "I would have been negligent in my job if I hadn't considered you a person of interest. But the evidence doesn't point toward you."

"It never did." She looked down at her lap.

"I know." He waited until she looked up again. "Look, staying by yourself isn't going to work. I'll have Bree come in and work the room, then pack up your things." He stood and pulled her to her feet.

"So where am I supposed to stay?"

"The safest place in the world." Adam let the room

door lock behind them and headed back to the motel office, still holding her hand.

This time she didn't pull away. "And that would be…?"

"Casa de Reed. Where else?"

Chapter Ten

Resting her head against the seat back in Adam's truck, Rachel closed her eyes. Everything about this day exhausted her. And now, Adam planned to keep her under lock and key at the Reed ranch. Not that she didn't appreciate the offer of a safe place to stay, but she wasn't some fair maiden, happy to be locked away while waiting for some prince to slay her dragons.

That, however, was a discussion for later. Now, with her emotions threatening her common sense, silence seemed the best option.

The truck bumped over a cattle guard, and she opened her eyes to a long dirt road ahead of them. When Adam followed a curve to the left, the view opened up, revealing a two-story rustic ranch house. Unfenced land stretched as far as she could see.

She struggled to keep undisguised amazement from her voice. "I knew y'all had a ranch, but does *all* of this belong to your family?"

Adam turned his head toward her and smiled. "Well, it's not a working ranch. The original property owner had planned to use it for cattle and horses but sold out instead. We call it a ranch, but it's really just a big piece of land with a house and some cabins." He lifted his shoulders, hinting at a shrug. "You like it?"

Aside from it being a country girl's dream, you mean? "I haven't seen enough of it yet to decide." She caught his disappointed expression from the corner of her eye.

He recovered in a flash. "I'll have to take you on a tour, then. We've got a decent-sized creek running through it, loaded with bass."

"That's nice." She wasn't about to let him know how much she loved this place. He might mistake her enthusiasm about his land for an interest in him. An interest she would deny until long after she left Resolute, when it would be too late to act on it. "Will I be staying in one of the cabins?"

Rolling to a stop in front of the house, he killed the engine and looked at her. "Absolutely not. You'd be too isolated. We'll all be staying in the main house for the duration."

"All?"

"You, me, Nate. Noah and Bree will probably be over more than usual." A dimple in his left cheek deepened as he smiled. "Safety in numbers and all that."

An only child, Rachel had lived with her mom until the day she married Eric. Then it was Eric, until the kids came along. Her comfort zone didn't allow for spending a lot of time with several adults on a regular basis. Even on the best of days at work, by the end of her shift she'd had her fill of people.

She pointed through the windshield at what looked

like a cabin sitting a short way off from the house. "What about that one? It's not isolated."

"No." His smile faded, and his dimple disappeared. "That's off-limits." His voice soft, he spoke almost as if in a trance, his blank stare a million miles, or maybe a million years, away.

"Well, then, I guess you better show me the big house. I really can't wait to see it." She got out of the vehicle and climbed the front steps.

By the time he caught up with her on the porch, his grin had returned. Her on-demand cheerfulness, a secret weapon at work to keep the customers satisfied, seemed to banish whatever dark memory had haunted him.

His change of mood lifted her own, her forced happiness segueing into reality. Despite her best intentions, a man's feelings mattered to her.

Damn it.

GRATEFUL FOR THE master bedroom with a private bath, Rachel lay on the bed, staring up at the ceiling. Bree had combed through the motel room for evidence, then delivered Rachel's belongings to the ranch. For now, she left it all in her suitcase, debating whether to sterilize or burn everything the creep had touched. The obvious option was sterilization: a new wardrobe was the last thing she could afford right now.

When Adam had mentioned rallying the troops, he hadn't been kidding. Nate had already been home when they arrived. Noah had left his vehicle at the justice center and had someone there give him a ride to Doc's so he could drive Rachel's car to the ranch. Not that she'd get to use it. Adam insisted that for her safety, he'd be chauffeuring her to work and anywhere else she might need to go.

Now the entire family, minus the still-honeymooning Cassie and Bishop, chattered and joked and argued downstairs.

She needed to go back down. Be sociable. Show gratitude for their willingness to take her in, circle the wagons around her, even play musical vehicles. After forcing herself to sit up, stand, then enter the master bath, Rachel splashed cold water on her face without bothering so much as a glance in the mirror. Her haggard face and bandaged head would only depress her.

Opening the bedroom door, she took a deep breath and headed for the staircase, while a fight about Adam raged between her heart and her brain. As she stepped off the final riser, she called for an internal détente, plastered a smile on her face and walked into the kitchen.

All conversation stopped, and all eyes turned to her.

"Don't mind me. Carry on with your conversation." Rachel noticed shot glasses on the counter near a bowl of cut limes and a saltshaker. "Where's the tequila?"

A flurry of movement and words surrounded her. Bree gave her a hug. Noah filled one of the tiny glasses with top-shelf tequila and set it in front of her. Nate pushed the limes and salt closer. Rachel licked her hand between her thumb and index finger, then sprinkled salt on it. Meanwhile, Noah filled the other glasses and the family readied to drink. When everyone had their glass in one hand, lime wedge in the other, the Reeds chanted a toast in Spanish, and they all licked salt, tossed tequila and sucked limes.

The back door opened, and Adam came in from the patio, holding a platter of grilled ribs. The aroma of seared meat tickled Rachel's nose, and her stomach growled.

Setting the platter on the counter, Adam smiled at her. "So they've already got you guzzling tequila, huh?"

"Wasn't like we had to twist her arm." Noah played bartender again, refilling the glasses and making sure Adam had one this time.

Rachel put down her glass. "Is this what passes as cocktail hour for you Reeds, or is this a special occasion?"

A chorus of *Cocktail hour!* made her laugh.

"You fit right in with this motley crew." Nate nudged her shoulder, and she couldn't help but smile.

Rachel helped Nate set the long table in the dining room while the others put final touches on side dishes, like scooping store-bought potato salad into a bowl and warming up canned baked beans.

Noah brought out an aluminum pan of ready-to-bake rolls. "We normally make everything from scratch, but this was short notice."

"Except dessert." Adam put the platter of ribs on a trivet.

"That's because Cassie's responsible for dessert." Nate returned from the kitchen with longneck beers for everyone. "And Cassie can't bake."

"*Bake?* Our dear sister can't even cook." Noah pulled out a chair next to the end of the table and held it for Rachel. "None of us would have survived if Adam hadn't taken over the meal-making when we were kids."

"Her only job at these dinners is to show up with a pie from the diner." Bree chuckled as she sat next to Noah. "Bless her heart."

By the time they finished dinner, Rachel had mellowed. They'd kept the conversation light, steering away from work topics and Rachel's situation. Between the excellent food, the tequila she wasn't used to and the fun company, today's upsetting events faded away. She pushed her chair back to rise and help clear the table.

Adam reached over and rested his hand on her arm. "No need to get up. I cook, the twins handle the cleanup. It's a division of labor that can't be fiddled with, or I'll have to start training them all over again."

Bree leaned back in her chair and patted her stomach with both hands. "Yep, and we womenfolk retire to the study with whiskey and cigars." She and Adam laughed when Rachel's eyes widened.

"As nice as that sounds, I believe I'm done with this day." Rachel stood. "If y'all don't mind, I'm off to bed."

Bree said good-night and wandered into the kitchen.

"Of course." Adam rose. "Is there anything else you need upstairs?"

"I don't think so. Thank you for inviting me to stay here." Her eyes locked with his, and her heart did a weird little extra beat. Maybe two.

"I'm glad you didn't put up too much of a fight." He smiled, drawing her gaze to his mouth.

A sudden desire to kiss that mouth swept over her, and she licked her lips.

"Looks like we've got a chocolate cream pie in the freezer," Noah yelled from the other room. "Y'all want a piece?"

The moment broken, Rachel turned away. "Good night," she said over her shoulder.

Adam's reply came as she stepped onto the top landing. "Sleep well." He stood at the bottom of the stairs, looking up at her.

She could only nod before making a hasty retreat into her room. Leaning back against the closed door, Rachel rested her hand over her left breast. The fast, irregular beats sent a message to her head:

Heart–1, Brain–0.

ADAM'S PULSE INCREASED as he read the background report on Richard Smith. His excitement always ratcheted up when clues in a case aligned. He buzzed Bree and told her to join him in his office.

Usually able to focus exclusively on a case, today he'd been distracted. Last night Rachel had finally seemed somewhat at ease. Chatting with his brothers, joking with Bree, her personality had dazzled him just as it had years ago. But it wasn't until after dinner, after he'd lost himself in her eyes, that he sensed the first stone coming down from the wall around his heart.

"Whatcha got, boss?" Bree slid into the chair across from his.

Blinking back to the present, Adam shifted his shoulders, attempting to ease the tension in his neck. "I think I'm one step closer to linking Eric to Smith."

Bree tapped her tablet to bring up the screen, then flipped open an old-school notebook and grabbed her pen. "Ready."

"Turns out our Richard Smith was released from prison three weeks ago."

"Ooh, ooh. Let me guess." She tapped her tablet a few times. "He was an inmate at the McConnell Unit?"

"Bingo." Adam pointed his finger at her. "Same unit Eric Miller served time in."

"They had to have met each other there." Bree scribbled notes on the paper pad. "Too much coincidence otherwise."

"No doubt, since they happened to be cellmates during the year before Eric's release."

She dropped her pen. "Hot damn!"

"When I called the prison, I also found out that Smith apparently saved Eric's life. He'd been beaten up several times. When an inmate came at him in the shower room with a handmade knife, Smith and members of the prison gang he'd joined intervened and the attacker wound up dead."

"Huh. So it was Smith in the shower with a shank." She smiled, obviously proud of her corny joke.

Adam ignored it. *Too much time with Noah.* "What I can't figure out is why Smith headed here after his release." Adam scrolled down on the computer screen, rereading details in Smith's background check.

Bree tapped her pen against her chin. “Maybe he needed a place to stay, and he figured Eric owed him.”

“He was originally from El Paso. He had to backtrack to Resolute if he was heading home.” Something didn’t ring true in the scenario. “Since you’ve got the notebook, take notes, okay?”

Bree flipped to a fresh page.

“Smith got out of prison one week before I saw him at the Dead End, fighting with Eric. Eric was last seen alive three days after the fight. The same day we found Eric’s body, Rachel’s apartment was broken into. Three days later we found Smith’s body.” He stared into space. “Now let’s run through the possibilities.”

Bree went first. “Smith could have been in town before you saw him. Could have been staying with Eric and lying low, or you just didn’t happen to see him.” She scribbled her thoughts on the pad.

“Eric could have been killed anytime between last Monday when he got out of jail and the day we found him.”

Bree glanced up. “So five days, right?”

Nodding, Adam continued. “Either Smith killed Eric, searched Rachel’s place, then was killed by an unsub, or the unsub did it all.”

“Or Smith killed Eric, and our unidentified subject did the rest.” Bree leaned back in her chair. “I think the first option makes the most sense. I just don’t see how we’re going to solve it until we figure out what everyone’s been looking for.”

“I’ll call the crime lab, see how much longer for the autopsy report and evidence list for Smith.” Adam snapped his fingers. "Has Doc sent over the security footage?"

"I picked it up on my way in this morning."

"Do the first pass on it, okay? Watch for the same vehicle going past the entrance more than once, especially yesterday. If it were me, I'd have made several passes before sneaking into the weeds behind the detached units."

Bree rose to leave but turned back at the door. "Want to have lunch at the diner? I love reviewing autopsies over a greasy burger and fries loaded with ketchup."

Adam grimaced at the image but agreed. "It'll give me a chance to check on Rachel. See how she's doing."

"Uh-huh." Bree added a little extra melody to the word.

"Professionally. You know, as a deputy does with a victim."

"Sure, boss. Whatever you say." She gave him a smug grin.

"You do know that your good habits are supposed to be rubbing off on Noah, not the other way around."

"You don't always get what you want." She laughed, then closed his door.

No kidding. He'd had a lifetime of experience learning that lesson.

Chapter Eleven

Adam sat in the last booth at the back of the Busy B, where no one could walk past and glimpse gruesome autopsy photos. He'd received the report just before noon, thanks to Brett putting a rush on it, and printed out a copy to review while he and Bree ate lunch.

Bree had stopped to talk to Marge on their way in, and now she slid onto the bench seat opposite him. "Marge says Rachel's doing okay, but… Ouch!" She leaned to the side and massaged the shin Adam had just kicked.

"Hi, Adam, Bree." Rachel stood next to their table with a pleasant smile on her face. She lifted the coffee carafe in her right hand. "Y'all want coffee or something cold to drink?"

Both deputies pushed their mugs toward her.

"How's your day going?" Curious about what Bree had started to tell him, Adam studied Rachel's expression.

"Oh, you know. Same old, same old." She set the carafe on the table and pulled her order pad from her apron pocket. "Your regular, or the special of the day?"

"Since when does Marge have specials?" Adam's brows skimmed toward his hairline.

"Since last week when she was shorthanded. She figured if she discounted one item, more people would order it and everything would be simpler." Her lips twisted to the side. "I heard it worked until she ran out of the special and everyone wanted the discount on whatever they ordered."

"Then, why is she still having specials?" Adam asked.

Bree jumped in before Rachel could answer. "What's today's special?"

"Tuna salad on white with potato chips." Rachel pulled her lips between her teeth, a sign Adam recognized as her attempt to not laugh. Her gaze traveled from Bree to Adam. "Same as it is every day. Marge found deals on industrial-sized cans of tuna and bulk potato chips from a restaurant supply store in Victoria, and a wholesale bakery overstocked with white bread. She loaded up on all three."

"That's a lot of tuna sandwiches," Adam deadpanned.

"Pretty sure she's going to be disappointed when people get tired of them." Rachel sighed. "But if we ever have a natural disaster around here, we'll be able to feed the first responders and volunteers."

"I wouldn't let that get out if I were you. It might be hard enough as it is to get volunteers." He laughed, and his chest warmed when Rachel joined in. "I'll have the club sandwich with fries."

Bree hadn't even opened her menu. "Bacon cheeseburger, extra bacon, extra cheese. With fries."

"In other words, your regular." Rachel raised a brow toward Bree, who just grinned.

Walking past the other booths on her way to the kitchen pass-through, Rachel stopped once, then visibly stretched herself taller. She turned to the closest booth with a big smile and said something to the two women sitting there. They shook their heads, then as soon as Rachel walked away, they leaned across the table toward each other, practically bonking their heads together.

"What the hell was that about?" Adam muttered.

Bree, who'd turned around to see what interested him so much, turned back. "That's what I was about to tell you when you kicked me. Marge said some of the customers are saying ugly things about Rachel. Like she killed Eric, Marge shouldn't let a murderer work here anymore, keep an eye out if she's carrying a kitchen knife." She took her anger out on the sugar packet she ripped open. "I tell you what..."

Adam's first instinct, to get up and start telling people off, came and went. But he continued to watch Rachel as she worked. Head held high, she shined genuine smiles on some diners while others received a polite, closemouthed grin. She didn't need his help in dealing with rude customers, even if their rudeness took shape as a personal attack on her.

"...turn on a dime against a person everyone loved last week."

Realizing Bree was still talking and obviously

angry, he frowned as if in agreement, then picked up the file at his side and handed it over to her. "Go ahead and read it. I saw a lot of the injuries firsthand at the scene."

While Bree skimmed the report, Adam leaned back and sipped his coffee, waiting for her reaction. It only took a minute before she looked up at him, her eyes wide and her mouth open. "Noah said the guy had been tortured, but he didn't tell me any details."

Adam nodded. "And according to the report, he had a recent bullet wound. I guess it just grazed him. I'm surprised the techs could identify the weapons so quickly. I figured a serrated hunting knife for the neck wound, but I couldn't even guess at the puncture wounds. I've never even heard of a Cyclone push dagger."

Bree glanced back at the picture of a spiraling three-blade knife with a T-handle. "We called them tridaggers in San Antonio."

"You ever see any when you were on the force there?" He welcomed any information the ex-cop could offer.

"Saw a few in evidence after gang busts. But an undercover officer I dated briefly told me a lot of cartel members carry them."

Adam signaled Bree to close the folder as Rachel approached with their food.

"Can I get you a refill on your coffee?" She brushed a tendril of hair away from her face with the back of her hand.

"Please." Adam smiled at her. "Looks like some

of your customers aren't being their usual gracious selves."

As she topped off their coffee, Rachel shrugged. "At least they're not calling me a serial killer after you found the second guy. You find out any more about him?"

"Working on it." Adam picked up half of his sandwich and took a bite. With a full mouth, he wouldn't have to evade Rachel's questions about the case.

She watched him chew for a moment. "Well, I better get back to it. A tuna special waits on no man." She gave him one of her sincere smiles before leaving.

"I guess the twins were right. You do have a serious crush on her." Bree popped a fry into a mound of ketchup, then into her mouth.

He set his sandwich down. "What are you talking about?"

Bree waggled a french fry at him. "Your whole face was smiling, even while you chewed."

A warm feeling took over his chest. And then…

Thud. Another stone rolled away.

RACHEL LEANED AGAINST the kitchen counter and took a sip of her Moscato, watching Adam search through an antique washstand the Reeds had repurposed into a liquor cabinet. She enjoyed a glass of the sweet, effervescent wine on occasion, especially at the end of a hard day.

"Finally." He straightened from his crouched position, holding up a bottle of sipping tequila in victory. "Sure you wouldn't rather have some of this? That wine is sweet enough to have as dessert."

"I'm good, thanks." She took another sip and smiled, proving that she was.

He'd picked her up at the diner after his workday ended, which meant she either sat in the diner waiting for several hours, or she worked a double shift. Needing the money, she'd worked straight through and felt it now in her lower back and left arm. Adam never had been much of a conversationalist. Between that and her exhaustion, the ride home had been a quiet one.

"Did your day improve after the lunch crowd left?" He leaned against a counter opposite her, swirling his glass.

An amused snicker escaped her. "The breakfast crowd consists of people who work near the diner and are in too much of a hurry to care who serves them, and old men who want to drink coffee and chew the fat for hours. I've been getting scowls from a few of the old men, but they've been flirting and joking with me for so long, I don't think they want to admit their judgment was wrong."

Adam chuckled. "That sounds about right."

Rachel smiled. "The dinner crowd, for the most part, didn't bat an eye. Now, lunch is a whole different thing. That's when the gossipmongers come in. Resolute's version of ladies who lunch and couples where the wife—" she held up her fingers as air quotes "—*whispers* to her husband every time I pass by."

"Hard to believe people you've known your whole life can turn on you just like that." He snapped his fingers.

Rachel didn't mention the Reed family, especially

Adam's sister and father, had come under scrutiny of their own not long ago. "The funny part of it is, they usually share their gossip with Marge. I mean, that's where she gets her best stuff. But when she gave the first customer to bad-mouth me the evil eye, no one's talking to her."

"I admired your determination to stay calm in there today. Not sure I would've if I were you."

Rachel snorted at the thought of Adam *not* being calm. "In all the years I've known you, I've never seen you lose your cool a single time." She looked up into his eyes. "You've always been the steady Reed, haven't you?"

"What do you mean?" His brows drew together.

"Cassie's the enforcer. Noah's the jokester. Nate's the rebel." She took a sip of wine, rolled it around in her mouth, tasting it before swallowing. "And you're the rock. The quiet, dependable, steady one."

Adam tipped his head to the side as if unable to comprehend her words. "I don't think… I've never thought of myself as…"

"Of course not. It's just who you are." Her candor surprised even her, and she raised her glass to her lips, trying to disguise the awkwardness of the moment. But her coordination failed her, and wine trickled down her chin and onto her waitress uniform.

By the time she'd set her glass on the counter and looked down in dismay, Adam was swiping at the splotch with a damp dish towel.

"Good thing it's white wine." Her eyes still downcast, she snorted a small laugh. "I seem determined to wind up with no clothes to wear at all."

Adam's head tipped up, and she raised hers until their eyes met, mere inches from each other.

"That would be a terrible thing." His voice carried a teasing tone.

Up close, his hazel eyes mesmerized her. With a greenish background and an explosion of gold around the pupil, they almost resembled a sunflower. A sunflower with a black hole at its center that pulled her and dared her to dive into its infinite expanse.

She'd never wanted to take a chance as much as she did right now. To leap without doubt, without worry, without fear. To give her heart another chance to experience what she'd missed out on with Eric. If she did, Adam might be the one she'd want to—

"When's Bree getting here with din—" Noah froze halfway through the kitchen archway. "Uh, sorry." He held up his hands in apology before a smirk lit up his face. "Didn't mean to interrupt anything." But instead of leaving, he leaned against the wall, surveying the two of them.

"I better go change, soak this in the sink." Rachel pulled the damp polyester away from her chest as she walked past Noah, her eyes avoiding him.

Behind her, Adam said, "I swear, Noah—"

"Hey. All I did was come into the food room at food o'clock. Not my fault you two can't keep your hands off each other."

Coming to a standstill, Rachel held her breath. She

shouldn't be eavesdropping, but her curiosity got the best of her.

When Adam didn't reply, Noah continued. "Seriously, bro, I'm just glad you're finally admitting you're in love with her. Looks like maybe she's warming up to you, too. But you can't get married before Bree and I do, or it'll screw up the alignment of the planets or something else crazy like that."

Rachel headed upstairs like a sleepwalker, unaware of anything around her. After closing the door behind her, she removed her uniform, draped it over the edge of the bathtub, then dropped onto a reading chair near the window.

What Noah said couldn't be true. Adam…in love… *finally*?

He was the one who'd barely spoken to *her* over a decade ago. And ever since returning from Sam Houston with his college degree, he'd been friendly but distant.

The very idea that he loved her was as preposterous as Noah's claim she was warming up to Adam. Sure, they were closer now than a month ago, but that was due to the circumstances. Kind of hard to live in the same house with someone like Adam and not at least think about what-if. Still… Could Noah read her better than Rachel could read herself?

She'd called Noah the jokester, so maybe he'd just been teasing. But what if he wasn't?

Her heart pounded a loud beat in her chest, and she took a deep breath, forcing it to calm down. Rachel shook off the thought. Either way, it didn't matter.

She'd already made plans for the rest of her life. And they didn't involve Adam Reed.

ALTHOUGH HIS HOUSEGUEST might not think it possible, Adam was perilously close to losing his cool and clobbering his younger brother. After spending a good portion of their lives in this house, the Reed boys were familiar with every sound it made, from squeaky floorboards to popping drywall. When Noah had finally stopped running off at the mouth, a silence descended.

And then Adam heard it. They both heard it. A slight shifting of weight on a hardwood floor. Noah's eyes widened into an expression of *oops*. Adam's narrowed into an expression of impending fratricide.

Rachel had heard every word before going upstairs.

Adam picked up the tequila bottle as if squeezing it to death by its neck and splashed a good-sized pour into his glass.

"Sorry. I thought she was gone." Noah grabbed another glass from the cabinet and set it next to Adam's.

Ignoring it, Adam picked up his and strode into the living room. He settled into his father's leather recliner, kicked up his feet and sighed.

With each sip, his anger at Noah faded a little. His brother could have been more discreet, but what he'd said was the truth. As much as Adam had denied still harboring feelings for her, it seemed he'd only been fooling himself. Well, himself and apparently Rachel.

But he hadn't planned to let Rachel in on this news. At least not yet. And definitely not in this way. Overhearing Noah might change Rachel's mind about everything. Test her trust in Adam, make her question his motives in insisting she stay at the ranch.

He needed to decide how to handle this. Pretend he didn't know she heard, or acknowledge it and pretend it wasn't true? At least, the part about how he felt about her. He didn't believe for one minute that she was falling for him. Not after all this time.

As if summoned by his thoughts, she came down the stairs and started for the kitchen.

"Rachel." He hoped to somehow alleviate this new awkwardness between them.

She turned, hesitated, then joined him in the living room. Her eyes didn't stay on any one thing for long, including him.

"I decided to check in with Mom and talk to the kids while I was up there."

Adam got to his feet. "Can I get you anything?"

"Not right now." She lowered herself on the edge of the couch as he retook his seat.

"So how are they doing? Enjoying San Antonio?" He sipped his drink.

"They're having a blast. Mom took them to the zoo today. She seems to have something planned daily to keep them out of Aunt Sylvie's hair as much as possible." Finally looking at him, she chuckled. "Apparently Sylvie didn't fall in love with them as quickly as Mom had hoped."

"It would take a cold, hard heart not to fall in love with those kids. You're lucky to have them." Adam held her gaze. "And they're lucky to have you."

Her cheeks blushed at the compliment. “Thanks. You sound like you’re a sucker for children.”

“Can’t wait to have a whole passel of my own.”

“A passel, huh?” She raised a brow.

“The way I see it, the more, the merrier.”

“Said by a man who doesn’t have any.” The corner of her mouth curled into a wistful smile. “Don’t get me wrong, I love my kids. But I draw the line at two.”

She couldn’t be serious. Could she?

“I have to admit, it surprised me to find out Eric wanted shared custody.” He set his glass on the oak side table.

“He didn’t really. He thought if he had the kids part of the time, he wouldn’t have to pay any child support.” She rolled her eyes. “He wasn’t a great father, but Brad always got so excited for his weekend with his daddy. I wanted consistency for them, whichever home they were at, but it never happened. No discipline, all the junk food and sugar Brad wanted. It was easier that way.” She shot him a look. “For Eric, at least.”

“What about Daisy? Was she happy to go, too?”

“She didn’t cry or scream when he took her. But more often than not she came home with diaper rash.” She paused, as if lost in thought. “Truth is, Eric never did seem too fond of babies. When Brad was born, Eric didn’t want anything to do with him. Not just the stuff like helping out, changing a diaper or getting up in the middle of the night with him. He didn’t want *anything* to do with him. So I doubt he interacted with his daughter much more than he had with his son at that age.”

“Well, he managed to wrangle you all the way to the

altar, so he must have had some good qualities." Adam couldn't even guess what those might be.

Rachel looked off, as if remembering a long-ago past. "He used to be sweet. Kind." She laughed at Adam's skeptical expression. "When I first met him, he treated me like a queen. And he always said he wanted kids. That's what really won me over, you know? I thought we both wanted the same things." She scooted farther back so she could lean against the couch cushions. "But he lied about everything. As soon as we moved into the garage apartment, he lost his job. We were supposed to pay Mom rent, but he knew she'd never kick me out. Then he lost interest in me the minute I became pregnant with Brad." A crooked smile curved her lips. "Color me foolish for thinking a Prince Charming could ever want someone like me. And color me *reckless* for thinking Eric could ever be anyone's Prince Charming."

"At least you tried to find happiness with someone you thought was the right person."

Unlike me, who's never even tried.

Maybe it was time to change that.

AFTER A DINNER of burgers and sides that Bree brought home from the diner, Rachel took her glass of wine out on the back patio. The evening air had cooled, but she'd changed into a long-sleeve top and jeans after her earlier wine mishap.

The large patio, perfect for a party, had a serious grill set up on one side and wooden picnic tables and benches on the other. Terra-cotta strawberry pots sat next to a brick wall where they'd get good light. Bending over to check for berries, the plants' scents informed her they held herbs instead. Adam must be one serious chef if he grew his own.

She set down her wine and wandered out onto a stretch of green grass surrounded by landscaping. As she walked a lap around the perimeter, she inhaled fragrant honeysuckle, night-blooming jasmine, sweet olive. Tipping her head back and gazing up at the sky, countless stars shined brightly.

Sensing a presence, Rachel spun around to find Adam walking toward her. "I hope it's okay that I gave myself a tour of your backyard."

"Of course. I don't spend enough time out here myself, since moving into my cabin." He took a deep breath of the floral-scented air. "Other than grilling, that is."

"You have an impressive herb garden." Strolling toward a tree, she sniffed, looked up and gasped. "An orange tree."

"Yep. And over there—" he pointed toward more trees growing beyond the grass "—are pear and apple trees. And we've got pecan trees all over our property."

"Put in a vegetable garden and some cows, you could practically live off the grid." The surprises from this man never ended. She glanced up, caught by his lingering gaze. A breeze lifted her hair off her shoulders and she shivered, more from Adam's closeness than the cool air.

Adam shrugged out of the light denim jacket he'd worn outside. Reaching behind her, he wrapped it around her shoulders, then pulled her even closer.

She went willingly into his arms. Into his warmth.

There was no future for them. She planned to leave Resolute for someplace with more opportunities, where she could earn decent money and provide a better life for her kids.

But she *wanted* to kiss him. She had for more than a decade. She'd dreamed about what might have been if he'd asked her out when they were teenagers. When life had stretched before them with endless possibilities. Only, he hadn't. And she'd stopped waiting for him, saving her dreams for her fantasies.

Lost in his gold-flecked eyes until the moment their lips met, Rachel murmured his name. She wrapped her arms around his neck as his mouth, warm and soft, brushed against hers. Teasing, caressing. But she needed more. Pulling him tighter against her, his lips firmed, their pressure igniting sparks deep within her.

They sparred with their tongues until his won, invading her mouth in the most delicious way. Then their lips met again, soft, gentle, but the growing passion within her spread like wildfire. A soft moan escaped her, and she knew kissing Adam Reed would never be enough for her.

"Y'all out here? Noah found another pie in the freezer. Want some?" Nate, this time.

Rachel's eyes popped open to find Adam watching her.

He leaned his forehead against hers and groaned. "I really think my parents should have stopped after two kids."

She got the giggles. Adam caught them. Each time they straightened and their eyes met, they burst into laughter until Rachel's sides hurt. Holding each other up, they made their way to the house.

"That wasn't the kiss it was supposed to be." Chuckling, Adam stopped at the kitchen door to catch his breath.

"Oh, I don't know. It's hard to beat romantic with a dash of humor." Although trying to make light of the situation, the words rang true to her. It *had* been a perfect kiss.

And she had to make sure it didn't happen again.

Before Adam had walked back into her life in a big way, her head and heart were on the same page. A bright white page, clean of financial troubles and man drama. But now, with every steady gaze, calm word and kind gesture, Adam ripped that page in two. Her head still longed for a fresh, new and untroubled start, while her heart began to color a vibrant picture. A picture so joyful it almost hurt. But she couldn't see the lines. She didn't know what shape those colors were creating.

And she was so very tired of being unsure.

Chapter Twelve

The next morning, Adam began the day in a great mood. Which lasted as long as it took for him to shower, dress and head downstairs.

Rachel had occupied his thoughts while trying to fall asleep the previous night. He'd gone outside just to check on her. The Reed family as a group could be overwhelming sometimes. Add in Noah's badly timed announcement regarding Adam's feelings about her, and he'd half expected her to flee the property.

Instead, they'd ended up kissing.

And what a kiss it was. Sweet. Passionate. Intense. He'd long imagined what kissing Rachel would be like, but reality far surpassed the fantasy.

And then…this morning happened.

While Adam filled his travel mug with coffee, Rachel walked into the kitchen. She returned his happy grin with a closemouthed hint of a smile.

"Morning. Sleep well?"

"Well enough, I guess." She pulled on a sweater over her diner uniform. "Ready to go?"

Snapping the lid onto his coffee, he studied her. This

wasn't the same Rachel as the one last night, the one who'd kissed with fervor, then giggled and laughed with joy.

"Something wrong?" he asked.

"No. It's just… I think we should keep things more…"

"In the friend zone?" He read it on her face and beat her to the punch.

"Exactly. Friend zone." Rachel beamed, apparently glad he understood, even if he didn't. Not really. "Uncomplicated. So much is going on right now—work, my classes, murders…"

"Sure. I get it." He forced a smile to match hers.

"Good, good. Well, I guess we should get going, then." She walked through the house, picked up her purse from the front hall table and strode outside.

Adam followed her, a voice in his head mocking him. His voice, but Bree's words from the previous day.

You don't always get what you want.

As SOMEONE WHO didn't talk a lot, Adam had never minded stretches of quietude. But today, even for him, the drive into town with his newly declared *friend* consisted of nothing but a long, awkward silence.

After dropping Rachel at the diner, Adam stopped by the office for the morning briefing and to pick up the key to Eric's apartment. He'd give the place one last walk-through before returning the key to Oak View's manager.

During the meeting, held in one of their conference rooms, Adam updated the other deputies on Richard

Smith's autopsy report. "We should get the rest of the reports sometime later today."

Sean stared at the photos being passed around. "That push dagger makes some ugly wounds."

"You should have seen the burns." As the only deputy besides Adam who'd seen the body firsthand, Noah narrated the photos. "And his hands? He cut each—"

"Noah. They've got the pictures, and I just read them the autopsy report." Adam sighed.

He called on Pete, Sean and Noah to each report on their cases next. As Adam's assistant, Bree had no cases of her own to report on, but he still did her the courtesy of calling on her.

"Dave?"

The only deputy yet to report, the man sat in his seat, arms folded over his skinny chest. A hush fell over the room, and the other deputies all turned to look at him at the last table. Ignoring them, Dave stared at Adam.

"Do you have any cases to report on, Dave?" Adam's patience with the disrespectful deputy had passed its *best-by date* and was quickly approaching *expired.*

"How am I supposed to have any cases to report on when you've stuck me in the bullpen every day to take calls?" Dave's face grew ruddy.

Refusing to engage, Adam said, "Okay, folks, this meeting is done. Let's get to work."

But Dave wasn't finished. Amid low murmurs and the noise from chairs sliding back from tables, he addressed Adam in a voice most likely heard all the way to the diner. "Exactly how long do you plan on punishing me for doing my job? For questioning a murder suspect you didn't have the nerve to question yourself?"

Like a children's game of statue, everyone froze.

"Admit it, Adam. You're abusing the privilege of your position by showing favoritism to Rachel Miller. You lost your objectivity because you have the hots for her."

Attempting to quell his anger before he spoke, Adam took a beat.

One long breath in and out later—*Thank you, Bishop, for your yoga-breathing techniques*—Adam had calmed down. Only a little, but enough.

"Deputy Sanders, let me clear the air on this once and for all." He paused while everyone nodded and sat back down. "I had arranged for Ms. Miller to come in so I could question her, which she willingly agreed to do. But when she got here, instead of knowing your place and not interfering in another deputy's case, you took her into an interrogation room and accused her of murder."

All eyes again turned to Dave.

Adam picked up where he'd left off. "*Without* reading her the Miranda warning, you tried to force her to confess to a crime she didn't commit." His ire resurfacing, Adam slammed a fist down on the podium in front of him. "Due to Ms. Miller's intelligence and knowledge of proper law-enforcement procedure, both of which you apparently lack, she held her ground, told you off and asked for a lawyer."

Noah put his hands together to clap, but Bree nudged him to stop, despite the satisfied smile on her face.

"Deputy Sanders, because you decided to make this

discussion department-wide instead of private, I'll respond in same. You violated procedures by accusing someone of a crime without advising them of their rights. You interfered in an ongoing investigation of which you weren't a part." He paused to inhale. "You have continuously treated other deputies with disrespect. Sheriff Reed and I have records of your negligence of duty. And you've shown a contemptible lack of respect to me as your commanding officer. As of this moment, you are no longer a Boone County deputy. I'll take your badge and gun now, before Pete and Sean escort you from the building."

Noah and Bree cleared the room before Dave began yelling obscenities and threats, refusing to surrender his badge and weapon. Pete and Sean had to lift and hold him while Adam took the items from him.

He walked with the three men to the front door, opening and holding it so Sean and Pete could walk Dave down the steps and to the parking area. Adam advised the guard, on duty whenever the building was unlocked, to lock the door if he saw Dave coming.

Stopping at Helen's desk, he massaged a hard knot in his neck.

"So we're short a deputy again, huh?" She peered at him over her reading glasses.

"But are we *really*?" Adam scoffed. "You know what my dad used to say."

They said in unison, "He's about as useful as a steering wheel on a mule."

Their laughter tapered off, and Helen's expression turned wistful. She and his dad had become good friends over the many years they'd worked together. Adam had a hunch that after his mom had disappeared, Helen had hoped the relationship might progress to something beyond friendship. But it wasn't in the cards for them back then.

Maybe he should read the cards for himself and Rachel, and decide if it was finally time to fold.

"COME WITH US, ADAM," Bree pleaded. "How can we celebrate being rid of Dave without you?"

"Y'all go on, have a good time at lunch. I'll stay here and handle calls." As glad as he was to be done with Dave, Adam didn't believe in celebrating another man's misfortunes. Karma and all that stuff Bishop always talked about. "Be back in an hour, and no booze."

"You're gonna be sorry. The Chute's having a lunch special on ribs today." Noah raised his brows. "Want me to bring you some takeout?"

"That's okay. But seriously, be back in an hour, 'kay? I want to swing by Eric's and Rachel's apartments again, make sure we didn't miss anything."

"From what Bree told me about the mess at Rachel's, I don't know how you could tell." Noah called to the others to wait for him. "Last chance. Helen said she'd hold down the fort."

"Get out of here before they leave you behind."

On his way to get a refill of coffee, Adam swung past Helen's desk. "I'm here and handling calls."

"As you should be." She nodded her approval. "Your sister would be proud."

"My sister's probably going to tan my hide for firing Dave while she's gone."

"Maybe you still haven't caught on, but Cassie doesn't want you walking in her shadow. She appointed you chief deputy because she knew you could handle the position, which includes making executive decisions." Helen *tsk*ed. "You were responsible as a ten-year-old, for heaven's sake. You never needed to be told to do something, you just did it. What I'm trying to tell you is hold on to your confidence and never doubt yourself. Admire your sister, but never fear her. The only thing she has on you is one year."

"Thanks, Helen. You always were my favorite, you know." He winked at her.

"Oh, get on with you." She blushed, then shooed him away with her hands.

Still smiling about getting Helen flustered, Adam got comfortable at his desk and turned on his computer. Forensics still hadn't sent the rest of the Richard Smith reports, so Adam wrote up a detailed record of what happened in the morning briefing. He added it to Dave's file, then glanced at his watch. Still a half hour before the gang got back.

Adam subscribed to several digital newspapers from around Texas. When he had time, he skimmed them, as well as online news services, to keep abreast of crimes in both large and small cities. He'd fallen behind lately, so now he opened the *Victoria Advocate*.

A lot of gang activity going on. He flipped through online articles, not surprised to see mentions of cartels, drugs, murders. He stopped at one with a different twist. According to the police, and with details from an unnamed witness, the Marea Cartel, working with the notorious Texas gang Los Malolos, had a vanload of money hijacked by two men. The gang had apparently been transporting a shipment of laundered money to be used in their joint drug trafficking and weapons exporting to Mexico.

The witness, a member of the gang who'd been injured, claimed two men opened fire on the small convoy as it rounded a curve on a remote road. All the gang members, save the witness, were killed, along with the head of the cartel's nephew who'd been supervising the transport.

One of the attackers, a Caucasian of average height and weight, made his getaway in the van, which was still full of an undisclosed amount of cash. The witness claimed the other man, described as a short, heavyset Caucasian, had been shot. But police only found one bundle of money, still in its homemade currency strap, near where a second vehicle had been parked.

So far, Boone County had managed to keep hardcore gangs from moving in, and their brushes with cartel activities had been handled. But Adam remembered Bree's mention of the triblade dagger being found among cartel members, and a chill ran up his spine.

They better stay out of Resolute if they know what's good for them.

He opened the *San Antonio Express-News* next. Always plenty of crime over in that direction.

BETWEEN THE LINGERING aches from her fall and the mental exhaustion from everything else in her life, Rachel had been ready to admit defeat to Marge and hang up her apron midafternoon. Her boss could last all day in the Busy B, most of it on her feet, and Marge was at least twice as old as her. Luckily, Adam had shown up early and saved her from that embarrassment.

Now, in her room, Rachel exchanged her uniform for jeans and a light crewneck sweater. She headed back downstairs and found Adam in the living room, reading a book.

"Mind if I have a glass of wine?"

He looked at her over the book. "Not at all. Help yourself." He again became engrossed in his reading.

Frustrated with the two quiet commutes today and now this, she went into the kitchen. *Help yourself.* Well, she was the one who wanted it this way, so why was she disappointed with the friend-zone way he was treating her?

She returned to the living room, glass in hand, and sat on the couch directly across from Adam.

"How was your day?" Friends at least talked, right?

With his eyes still on the book, he held up one forefinger in a *wait a minute* gesture. He turned the page, continued to read. Rachel sipped her wine, unamused by his rudeness. He finally slipped a bookmark between the pages, closed the book and set it aside. *Then* he looked at her.

"Sorry, just wanted to finish that chapter." He surprised her with a smile. "My day was interesting. How was yours?"

"Just another day." She arched a brow. "Good book?"

Adam nodded. "Very. Do you read much?"

"I do when I have the time. I guess you don't remember that about me." In school, she had *always* had a book tucked under one arm, ready to read a few pages while waiting for the next class to start.

"That was a long time ago." His attention shifted to a speck of invisible lint on his shirtsleeve. Pushing the recliner's footrest down, Adam leaned forward, resting his elbows on his knees. "I did another walk-through of Eric's apartment today. And yours."

"Was that the interesting part?" He wouldn't have brought it up if there was nothing to tell her.

"Yes, but there were other interesting parts, too. I'll tell you about those later." He met her gaze, his expression serious. "Both apartments were searched again."

Rachel's eyes widened. "Did that Smith guy go through them a second time before he was killed?"

Adam shook his head. "Both resembled the search at your motel room. Organized. Efficient. Everything had been placed in careful groupings. As if he stacked the items as he searched them to avoid picking them up again. But at Eric's, this time vent covers were also removed and the carpet had been pulled up along the walls."

"Did you find anything new at my place? To indicate who he is?" A new thought struck her. "Was Mom's house searched?"

"Unfortunately, yes."

Rachel closed her eyes. How would she tell her mom about this?

"He, whoever he is, went in through a back window." Adam lifted his hands, as if trying to allay her fears. "I called Jeb's Glass Repair and waited there until he finished replacing it."

No matter that Rachel's mind was still reeling, Southern manners kicked in. "Thanks."

"It wasn't ransacked like the first searches," Adam went on, as if he hadn't heard her. "But it seemed thorough. I didn't find anything at your mom's or your place to even hint at who he is." He rubbed his hands together, almost as if fortifying himself to continue. "But at Eric's, a pile of papers on his kitchen table had been spread out."

"What kind of papers?"

"Your divorce papers. The child-custody agreement. Bank statements for an account in both your names."

"Those aren't surprising. I mean, other than the fact Eric actually kept copies of important papers."

Adam blew out a breath. "The point is, whoever broke in last found these papers somewhere. Forensics, Noah, me, none of us came across any papers when we searched his place." He rubbed the back of his neck, as if it were knotted with tension. "Your name and address were on those papers. Along with your kids' names. If Smith didn't give you up to this second perp, I think that's how he found his way to your apartment. And we don't know what else he might have learned about you."

"But how did he find me at the motel? I didn't even poke my head out the door until you picked me up for my medical follow-up."

"I talked to Missy Jenkins while I waited for the

glass guy. She told me she saw a man walking down your driveway Monday afternoon. She met him on the sidewalk and asked what he was doing there."

Rachel shifted on the couch, her anxiety returning.

"He told her he was the adjuster from your insurance company. Said he had an appointment to meet you at your apartment so he could settle your claim, give you a check. He even gave her a business card from an insurance company. Said if he didn't meet with you that day, it would be weeks before he could make it back to Resolute."

"But insurance claims are mostly handled online." Rachel stopped short of telling him she had no insurance.

"Apparently, Missy doesn't know that. She told him he'd just missed you, but he could probably catch you at the diner. When he asked what time you'd be back home in case you weren't at work, she mentioned you were staying at Doc's."

Rachel's chills worked their way inside, poking icicles into every single muscle and bone in her body. "How did Missy know I was staying at Doc's? How did he find out which room I was staying in?"

"I'd guess Missy found out through small-town gossip. As to how he figured out which room, I'm not sure. But I'm not going to stop until I find this guy. Until then, I promise to keep you safe."

She gave him a weak smile. "I think I'll hold you to that."

"Good." He stood. "I'm getting a drink. Can I bring you a refill?"

Fearful images of a lethal assailant bombarded her mind. She looked at her wineglass, which she'd barely touched. Bringing it to her lips, she tipped her head back and drained it. "Why don't you just bring the whole bottle?"

Chapter Thirteen

Another day went by with little movement on the Miller case. Adam finally got the rest of the reports on the Smith murder. Skimming through the evidence items he'd already seen, he stopped at the entry for the paper found in the dead man's pocket. An enlarged picture of it showed that the strip was actually two pieces, held together by what looked like an adhesive label. He read the description: *One currency strap, plain white paper, homemade.* A side note explained the homemade assumption: *Banking institutions use straps that are colored based on the dollar value of the bills.*

Adam pressed the bases of his palms into his eyes. *Where did I see that?* He pulled up files on his computer and skimmed through one before it dawned on him. He retrieved the electronic copy of the *Victoria Advocate* he'd read and located the article about the money heist tied to the cartel in Mexico and a gang in Texas.

...police only found one bundle of money, still in its homemade currency strap, near where a second vehicle had been parked.

And Bree had found two of those papers at Rachel's.

The excitement of the discovery battled with its ominous meaning. Adam called the Victoria Police Department, identified himself and asked to speak to someone with knowledge of the cartel van heist. After sitting on hold for several minutes, the line was picked up.

"Detective Solis." The man had a deep voice, filled with impatience.

"This is Chief Deputy Adam Reed, Boone County. I read an article recently about a cartel van full of laundered money being hijacked—"

"Yeah, that's my case." He snorted. "Or one of the many. Whatcha need?"

Adam's knee bounced beneath his desk, excitement kicking in. "I've had a couple murders in Resolute the past week or so. Found one of those homemade currency straps in the pocket of one of the deceased."

"No kidding. Got a description of the guy?" From Solis's tone, his interest had just ratcheted up.

Adam read off what he had for Richard Smith.

"That sounds like it could be one of the two who attacked the van. Damn SOBs. I can't believe they took out a whole group of Los Malolos. I mean, that gang picked the right name for themselves. They are *bad* dudes."

"I've been having some other odd stuff going on around here. Someone searched the apartment of the man we think Smith killed, as well as the man's ex-wife's home."

"Give me your email address."

Adam rattled it off to him.

"Okay, I'm sending you a police sketch of the guy our witness described. See if it looks like your Richard Smith. I'm searching for Smith in our records, too." Solis pounded on a keyboard with what sounded like just two fingers.

Adam opened the attachment and blew out a breath he'd been holding. The drawing was a close likeness to Smith. "I think that's him."

A long whistle came through the phone, and Adam pulled the receiver away from his ear. "What?"

"You do a background on Smith?" Solis asked.

"Of course. That's how I'm tying our two dead guys together. Smith and Eric Miller shared a cell in McConnell. Smith was locked up for possession with intent to distribute."

"Yeah, but that ain't exactly the whole story. I just had to open up a special file on him. Seems at one time he'd been working as a confidential informant for one of our guys in narcotics. He was in Los Malolos, and they were working a big deal with the Marea Cartel. The deal went south, and the gang left Smith holding the bag. He went to prison, vowing he'd make Los Malolos pay. Guess he made good on his word."

"Except, now he's dead."

"Yeah, that was the next thing I was about to tell you. We got word a few days ago that the head of Marea went nuts when he heard his nephew died in the gunfight, and sent a hitman to find the money and make whoever took it suffer. Sounds like Smith took care of the other guy for leaving him behind and taking off with the money, and the hitman took care of Smith. Can you confirm Smith was tortured?"

Adam's nostrils flared at the memory of burnt flesh and missing fingers. "Oh yeah. No doubt about that."

"Well, there you go. Won't know for certain unless we can match up some details between our two departments, but I'd bet that's how it went down. Now, there's just one last thing he's after."

"The money," Adam muttered.

"Yep. And he most likely won't stop killing until he finds it."

SINCE IT WOULD be just her and Adam for dinner that night, Rachel asked Lee, the Busy B cook, to prepare two take-out meals before she clocked out.

When she walked out of the diner, balancing them, as well as a box of brownies and a peach pie, with her purse hanging in the crook of her elbow, Adam jumped out and rushed to help.

"I figured we'd just pick up shrimp po' boys on the way home." He held the baked goods while she placed the meals on the back seat. "But this smells like a much better idea."

"Of course it does. It was *my* idea." She set the pie next to the meals, and as she took the brownies from him, the box slipped from her grasp and landed on the pavement, followed by her purse.

Rachel retrieved the brownies, put them in the vehicle and closed the door. Then she crouched to pick up her purse, which had managed to flip upside down and dump its contents on the street.

Adam squatted to help her pick up the loose items. "What's this for?" He held a lone key, studying it.

It took a moment for Rachel to remember where the key came from. "Oh. That's the key Missy found in the can of formula Mom gave her."

Adam's eyes flicked to hers. "What?"

With everything else back in her purse, Rachel stood. "When Missy took the kids last week, Mom gave her one of Daisy's diaper bags with a partial can of formula in it. The day I got my car, Missy told me she found the key in the can and thought it might be to something important. I tossed it in my purse and forgot about it."

Straightening to his full height, Adam turned the key over in his palm. "How did a key wind up in the formula can?"

Distracted by how well his broad shoulders filled out his uniform, Rachel shrugged. "I didn't put it there, and I know my mom would never do something like that." She opened the front passenger door, more than ready to get off her feet and stop thinking of Adam in any way other than a friend. "The only possibility I can come up with is that it was in the partial can that was in Daisy's bag at Eric's. Brad probably put it in there when he was playing." She waved her hand in the air, dismissing the key and thoughts about Adam's physique. "It's probably just an extra key to Eric's apartment."

"This isn't a front-door key." Adam held it up so she could see it. "It has the manufacturer's name on it, and that company only sells padlocks. We use them on the ranch."

Realizing Adam's continued interest in the key might be more than curiosity, she frowned. "And...?"

"And I need to tell you what I discovered today." He closed her door and climbed in behind the wheel. Glancing at her as he started the engine, he said, "After we get home. It's a lot. Speaking of a lot, why brownies *and* a pie?"

"I already had the day-old brownies packed up when Marge said she made too many peach pies. Told me to take one so it wouldn't go to waste. Figured I'd stick it in the freezer for now."

"Good idea. Can never have too much pie around the Reed household."

An energy enveloped Adam like an incandescent shroud, sparking and shimmering. Excited, nervous, maybe both. He obviously thought the key was what everyone had been searching for, and Rachel called on a patience she rarely possessed to remain silent during the drive home.

Odd how she referred to the Reed ranch as home after just a few days. As uncomfortable as she'd expected to be there, that hadn't come to pass. The three Reed brothers, and Bree of course, made her feel like part of their family. And she kinda liked it, despite herself.

"WHERE ARE WE GOING?" Rachel asked as they drove past the main house and deeper onto the property.

"Figured we could switch it up a little." Adam winked. "I've got a better view from my back deck to catch the sunset."

Intrigued by the opportunity to see where he lived when not babysitting her, she took in the scenery during the short trip. When they arrived at a rustic log cabin, Adam carried the takeout, and Rachel followed with the brownies as he led the way around to the back. Climbing several steps to the deck, Rachel couldn't help but be amazed by the wide-open view.

"Have a seat." He indicated two chairs, pulled up to a small table where he set the food.

While Rachel unpacked their meals, Adam retrieved a pitcher of iced tea from his refrigerator and two glasses.

As they ate, he told her about the currency strap in Smith's pocket and the ones he must have dropped when he'd broken into her place. Then he filled her in on the newspaper article about the cartel heist.

He repeated his conversation with the police detective in Victoria, each word, every phrase, causing her more distress. The two men had put the pieces together with logic and information, and she had to accept that Eric had taken part in a crime which had eventually led to his death.

"I just don't understand why he would have done it. Gotten mixed up with the cartel and gangs?" Rachel set her fork down.

"I may have figured that out, too. When I talked to the guy at the prison, he mentioned that Smith had saved Eric's life. A prison gang had planned on killing him, and Smith pulled in some of his *associates* and stopped it. I could be a hundred percent wrong here, but I think Smith told Eric he owed him. Smith wanted revenge on Los Malolos, and he came after Eric to help him pull it off."

"But Eric could have just said no. Refused. Even reported Smith to you if he had to." Rachel tucked her hair, lifting in the evening breeze, behind her ears. Why would he have put her and her family in danger?

"According to Solis, Smith had been a member of Los Malolos. Because he was on the outs with them when arrested, he worked a deal for protection from another prison gang. Outside at the Dead End, I got a hinky feeling about him just by looking at him. I seriously doubt Eric had a choice."

"And if he hadn't driven off with the money, leaving Smith behind, everything would have worked out? They'd have split the money and gone their separate ways?"

"I'm not sure it would have wound up like that." Adam glanced at her, and she caught a look of sympathy in his eyes. "Smith probably wouldn't have been eager to share his new fortune with a guy he hadn't seen in years. He might have killed Eric either way."

"So to summarize, Smith killed Eric, a cartel hitman tortured and killed Smith, and now the hitman is after the money."

"Close. The hitman has no idea where the money is, so technically, he's after you."

"But I don't know where the money is, either." Huddling farther into her jacket, Rachel shivered. "Too bad *close* only counts in horseshoes and hand grenades."

"Which brings us to…" he stretched out his leg and

worked his hand into his front jeans pocket, then held up the key "…this."

"You think that key unlocks whatever Eric hid the money in?"

"I do."

"Even if it does, that gets us no closer to the money. There are a million places he could have hidden it in Boone County alone. For all we know, it's in Victoria, San Antonio, anywhere."

"O ye of little faith." He held the key in front of his face and examined it in the fading light. "I'll bet anything this key unlocks a padlock on a storage unit. And since no one has found the missing van yet, I'm guessing the unit is large enough for a vehicle." He popped that doggone dimple at her again. "All I need to do is have everyone in the office call storage facilities with those types of units."

Rachel's optimism had dwindled the more she learned from Adam. "So I just need to avoid any cartel hitmen who torture before they kill until you happen to find the one storage facility with the one unit with the one lock that particular key unlocks. In—what?—over a thousand square miles?"

It seemed like a hopeless task, and it grew harder to hide her fear now that she understood exactly what danger she might be in. Adam must have seen it on her face because he reached over from his chair and took her hand.

"I asked you once before if you could trust me, and you said you could." He met her gaze and entwined his fingers with hers. "I'm asking you to trust me again."

Rachel stared into his eyes, their calm intensity relaxing her. Used to taking care of herself, she was smart enough to accept help in a situation like this. "I trust you." She squeezed his hand, noticing how well it fit with hers.

Chapter Fourteen

"Unless you're in the middle of an investigation that can't wait a couple of hours, I want you all calling storage facilities this morning." After explaining the importance of the key in the morning briefing, Adam switched up assignments. "I'll start with Boone County. Noah and Pete, start with Victoria as the center and work your way out to the county line. Sean, Bree, you two take DeWitt County, moving north toward Bexar County and San Antonio. Keep a list of any storage facilities who don't answer and pass them to Helen. She'll keep trying to reach them."

The clatter of chairs sliding and boots thumping as everyone left the meeting only served to ramp up Adam's energy. His gut told him they would find the stolen van, as well as the money. The only problem after that would be making sure the news reached the hitman before *he* reached Rachel.

Waiting for his computer to wake up, Adam found it hard to push her image from his mind. He'd dreaded telling her everything he'd learned yesterday. About Eric's part in the heist. About a cartel hitman coming after her. But she'd taken it better than expected. Definitely scared, but not traumatized. Determined to carry on instead of hiding in a closet. He admired that about her.

That, and a whole lot more. He just wished their first kiss hadn't sent her scurrying for the friend zone. He understood her reluctance to cross that line any further than they'd already flirted with.

She was leaving. Leaving her dead-end job, her disappointments and regrets, and forging a new life for herself and her kids somewhere else.

And he would be here. He had no intention of ever moving away from Resolute.

It wasn't fair for either of them to ask for more from each other. Not with their end already in sight.

And yet he yearned for it. More, that is. More time, more conversations, more Rachel in his life.

His monitor screen came to life, and Adam began his search. Boone County might be small, but there were a surprising number of storage facilities located between its lines. A lot of them housed boats, and a lot of them had recorded greetings answering their phones with invitations to leave a message. He worked his way through the list alphabetically, emailing Helen the contact info for the ones he couldn't reach.

At noon Noah stuck his head into Adam's office. "We're hungry and ordering pizza. You want any?"

Adam listened to another call go straight to voice mail. He left a message and hung up. "Yeah, and the department will spring for it since y'all are planning on working through lunch. Check with Helen, okay? She may want some, too."

"Sounds good."

As the next phone number rang in his ear, Adam thought about how grateful he was to work with this group of deputies.

Four hours and too many pizza slices later, Adam punched the number for a facility in Hudsonville, about twenty miles northwest of Resolute. The tip of his forefinger had gone numb, and he worried about wearing off his fingerprint.

"Vic's Self Storage. What can I do for you?"

"Is this Vic?"

"No, this ain't Vic. Vic's dead." The man on the other end sighed as if he had to answer that question a lot. "What do you want?"

Adam gave his own sigh. "I need to speak to the owner or manager."

"You're speakin' to 'em both. Name's Hank."

"All right, Hank, this is Boone County Deputy Adam Reed, and I need to find out if you rented a unit recently to an Eric Miller."

"We don't give out that kind of information without a warrant, so—"

"Miller is deceased, and his ex-wife has the key to the unit."

"Don't matter. If she's not listed as having authorized access, as well as the gate code, she'd have to show up with a probated will proving she inherited the contents."

"Okay, then, I'll have a warrant when I come up there. But if I can't have one specifically for Eric Miller's unit because you won't tell me if he rented one, you'll be opening every single door on that property."

Adam's tone, laced with the frustration of the past several hours, was met with silence.

He continued. "So you can either upset one dead customer or a whole bunch of live ones. Your choice."

"Hang on a sec." The line went to old-time country on-hold music.

Adam tapped his fingers on his desk to the beat, trying to keep his blood pressure from rising. Some of Rachel's skepticism had started bleeding into his certainty after so many calls.

The line clicked over. "Yeah, rented him a unit a few weeks ago."

Adam's fingers froze. *Finally.*

"He didn't want to put it in his real name, but we got rules, y'know," Hank continued. "Needed his license to set it up."

Grabbing a pen, Adam readied for all the information Hank could give him before he requested the warrant.

"Did Miller rent an interior or exterior unit?"

"Exterior, that's all we got. Unit 86."

"You have security cameras on your property?" Adam crossed his fingers for this one. Three weeks was a long time to keep footage.

"Yeah, but just for the front gates and the office. Motion activated, and we store it on a computer. You can take a look at it when you get here." The man moved his mouth away from his phone and spat what Adam assumed was chewing tobacco. "And don't forget your damn warrant." The line went dead.

Adam headed for the bullpen. "I found it."

The other four deputies, all holding receivers, two talking into them, hung up.

"Where is it?" Sean picked up a half-eaten slice of pizza and took a bite.

"Hudsonville," Adam said. "I have to request a warrant from Judge Harmon."

Four sets of eyes went to the wall clock.

Sean swallowed. "You better put your running shoes on, boss. You know how the judge is on Friday afternoons."

Judge Harmon usually took his sweet time with warrants, and a request coming in this late in the day at the end of the week most likely wouldn't be answered before Monday.

He went back to his office and prepared the warrant and affidavit, laying out all the facts in detail. Instead of sending it electronically, which the judge preferred, Adam printed it out and jogged over to Harmon's office on the other side of the justice center.

The judge had already left. With his office locked and his administrative assistant gone, Adam trudged back to his desk. He tried reaching both the judge and his assistant by phone, with no luck. He'd learned years earlier not to try Harmon at home on weekends. But he knew where to find him tomorrow morning, and the judge wouldn't throw a hissy fit in public.

"BUT WHY CAN'T we go now?" Rachel's stomach, a mess of knots and anxiety ever since Adam told her the so-called good news that he'd found Eric's storage unit, tightened even further.

They'd driven to his cabin again after work, intent on enjoying another sunset. But at this moment, she wasn't enjoying anything.

"We need a warrant." Adam looked at her as if she'd asked what color the sky was.

And in a way, she had. Adam was a law-enforcement officer, a by-the-book man who had rules to follow, procedures to guide him. She knew even before he opened his mouth what the answer to her question would be.

But she wasn't in law enforcement. She was a woman with a stack of bad choices behind her and two children to look after.

When Adam first told her his idea about the key and the money and the theft, she'd nodded along. After all, it had sounded logical. But still, she hadn't given it much credence. Eric Miller had been a deplorable husband and a distant father—but a thief? Of *cartel* money?

Maybe her mind was trying to prevent her heart from realizing just what a monumentally bad choice she'd made all those years ago. And yet Adam, looking every inch the man she should've chosen, stood here proving to her the danger was real.

"Can't we call the judge and..." She trailed off at Adam's expression. Even she knew that Judge Harmon had only one speed with which he lived and worked. He probably signed warrants the same way he plowed through the many club sandwiches Rachel had served him at the Busy B. In a deliberate and unhurried manner, taking up Rachel's time and a table for a two-dollar tip.

"I'm here, Rachel." Adam stepped forward, as if he'd just realized the reason for her sudden inability to speak. "I've got you. You're safe."

"Am I?" The question was out before she could stop it. She swallowed the large lump of emotion that threatened to spill over at any minute.

She was stronger than this. She'd just had a long day and was tired. Between morning and afternoon shifts, Marge had taken her to the doctor to get the staples removed from her head wound. Still, her hands shook.

Adam took her hands in his. "You're cold."

They both knew she wasn't. Her hands were just as warm as his, but she was grateful for the lie. Made her feel more in control of a situation where she had none.

"Come on inside." He pulled her hands toward him, setting her feet to shuffling over the wooden porch.

Entering Adam's cabin helped ease some of the fear inside her, as if subconsciously she knew she was heading for safety.

The dark wood beams, the polished wide-planked floors, the sparse but homey furnishings seemed to welcome her.

A large leather chair with an ottoman sat in the corner of the room off the kitchen, a precarious stack of books resting on a small trestle table beside it. The image of Adam, legs up after a long day of ensuring Resolute's safety, reading from one of those books, sprang crystal clear to her mind. As did the image of her, just a few feet away on the love seat near the fireplace, working on her schoolwork from a laptop perched on the squared armrest.

The sounds of Brad and Daisy, laughing as they ran and played outside, the ongoing soundtrack to their lives.

Her heart sped up for a different reason than fear.

Behind her, Adam closed the door. The click of it closing in the frame acted as a release valve for her pent-up tension.

Here was safe because Adam was safe. At least that's what her heart, the muscle hammering away at her rib cage, seemed to scream with every beat.

But was he?

Her mind had a list of reasons why he might not be. A list that grew longer and longer as Eric's life choices continued to haunt her. A list that would derail her well-planned future.

"Hey, now." Adam's arm came around her, pulling her back against his front, holding her tired, limp body against his strong, hard frame. "Everything's going to be okay."

She dropped her head back on his shoulder, tilting her chin up to look at his profile. "Is it?"

"Yes." He kissed her temple.

More tension left.

"First thing tomorrow, I'll track down Harmon at his church's Saturday pancake breakfast and have him sign the warrant. He won't create a stir in front of his cronies, so trust me, he'll hop to it."

The thought of the judge hopping at all got a small chuckle out of her.

"Then I'll collect my backup, and we'll head straight to Hudsonville and find out what's in Eric's storage locker."

His five-o'clock shadow grazed her ear.

"With any luck, by this time tomorrow, the news will be out about the money, you'll be safe, and Martina and the kiddos will be headed back to Resolute."

Another kiss to her temple, another tickle of whiskers, and a new kind of tension started to unfurl inside her. "Is that right?"

"Mm-hmm." He tightened his hold around her, her bottom snug below his belt.

Her troubles seemed to melt farther away with every second he held her. She knew it was dangerous, but she couldn't pull away. She forced her eyes, which wanted to close to savor his touch and warmth, to stay open, as she tried for a change of topic. "I like your house."

"I like you in it." His breath against her skin sent goose bumps trailing in its wake.

So much for a new topic.

"You do, huh?" Unwittingly, Rachel arched her back, pressing herself against him.

"I'd like you even better in my bedroom." His voice, deeper now than a moment ago, set fire to all her reasons why this would be a bad idea.

"I kinda figured you had an ulterior motive for keeping me safe on your property." She smiled at him over her shoulder. "Show me."

"I can't."

Rachel stilled, an unexpected, acute stab of disappointment jolting her to her senses. "You can't?"

"Nope." Adam's lips found her ear. "Bedrooms aren't for *just* friends." He nibbled.

Ah. With those words, instead of annoyance, a thrill shot through her. He wasn't so unaffected by her request to remain friends as he acted. With his arms around her and the stiff welcome message pressing against her bottom, Rachel's womanly powers flexed their long-unused muscles.

Slowly turning so that their bodies continually brushed against each other, Rachel faced Adam, her hands sliding up his chest. "Is that so?" Passing his shoulders, her arms rested behind his head, their pressure causing him to curl forward, lowering his head to hers.

"Yeah." He dipped farther, kissing the end of her nose.

Rising on her tiptoes, she kissed him back, hers landing on the corner of his mouth. A glance in his eyes, now dark with passion, sent another thrill through her. "Who said we're friends?"

"You did."

They stood at the threshold of no return, and Rachel desperately wanted to step through. Her mind tried to speak up, to shout over the hard beating of her heart. Warn her that her heart's track record was proof that this, this next step with Adam, was not a good idea.

She couldn't hear it. But she could feel the rightness of being in Adam's arms, the heat from his touch warming a place in her heart that had long been cold.

"That was then." With one hand, she traced a line along the ridge of his brow to his temple, down his cheekbone to the place she'd kissed. "Tonight, I'm not *just* your friend." And with her other hand, she urged his mouth to hers.

As slow as they started, once their lips touched, their passion ignited into something fierce and torrid. Jackets were shucked where they stood, clothes peeled off as Adam guided her through the cabin and down a small hallway to his bedroom.

By the time Rachel's back hit the bedcovers, it was bare. Standing between her legs, Adam's eyes roamed over her. From her hair, spread wild around her, to her breasts, rising and falling as her breath quickened with desire. Leaning his hard, well-muscled chest over her, he slid his hands beneath her hips, palming her butt, before sliding them up and curling his fingers into the back waistband of her jeans and panties. A few tugs later and she was laid bare for him to feast on.

And feast he did. Dropping to his knees, he worshipped her. In this moment, with his mouth against her, his tongue finding her pleasure spots, Rachel could believe that Adam had loved her since high school. She could feel that love with every nibble, every kiss and suck and twirl, until her legs threatened to lock around his neck as her ecstasy crested, tossing her over the summit and into free fall.

Every muscle contracted as fire raced through her veins and sparks of desire sizzled through her body like fireworks. And then her body dropped, became liquid. "Adam." Her voice was soft and low, unrecognizable to her own ears. Had she ever been so satisfied? So filled with passion?

It wasn't until she registered the crinkle of plastic as a condom wrapper that her mind began to focus once more. Lashes fluttered open as she pulled herself farther up the bed to where Adam stood, nightstand drawer open, condom in hand.

"Let me." She reached for the open package without thought, without any uncertainty, though she'd never put one on a partner before. Always too unsure of herself and her desirability.

Even during her marriage, Rachel never found the self-confidence that she seemed to have in this moment with Adam.

His nostrils flared as he handed her the condom, his desire seemingly checked—but barely. Taking it from him, she placed it on the bed beside her and swung her legs over the side.

"Rachel?"

Her eyes met his, and knowing full well the impact she was making, Rachel licked her lips. Slowly. Thoroughly.

Adam's eyes widened, and his jaw clenched. She spared him a smile before taking hold of his hard length and opening her mouth.

Do not embarrass yourself.

That was all Adam could tell himself as the woman he had loved for as long as he could remember slid her tongue down the length of his hard shaft.

It took all his mental strength to ensure his knees didn't buckle as the warm, wet sensation of her mouth began to suck.

"Rachel." His fingers threaded through her hair.

Rachel groaned, rewarding him with its vibrations. With one hand, she worked what she couldn't fit into her mouth, with the other she grabbed his rear, holding him to her.

She didn't need to worry: he wasn't going anywhere. This was where he wanted to be. Where he had always wanted to be. With her. Rachel. The woman who had the power to ease and unsettle him with one look. Who made his life brighter and fuller. Who could bring him to his knees, as she was proving now, every time her head pulled and bobbed before him.

In the back of his mind he knew they weren't going to last. That Rachel, a bright, shiny star held back too long by her unfortunate ex, was set to shoot off out of Resolute for bigger, greater things.

But he had now, and he had here, and he was going to take it.

His toes dug into the rug, and his spine began to stiffen.

"Rachel, wait." He stepped back, nearly coming undone as her lips, wet and puffy, stayed parted.

Blinking up at him, as if she, too, had been lost in the sensations, she frowned. "What—"

He pushed her back, laying her sideways across the bed, uncaring about pillows and blankets and small comforts. He barely had enough thought process left to grab the condom and put it on in record time before he slammed home.

And home was exactly what it was.

Rachel. *Home.*

The word hit him with each thrust. With each moan of pleasure from Rachel's mouth and every drag of her nails against his back.

Never mind tomorrow. Never mind the rest of his life. He would take what she gave him, and he'd make sure she lived with no regrets.

Crying out each other's names, they came—curled together as if trying to burrow into each other's hearts.

Minutes passed, and their labored breaths slowed as their sweat cooled. Adam found strength enough to yank the covers down from under them and tuck them both in before his body began to shut down from the pleasure they'd just shared.

With their bodies entwined, Adam had one last thought before his mind drifted into sleep. *No regrets.*

At least, not about Rachel.

DRIVING INTO TOWN to find the judge the next morning, Adam hummed a happy tune. Rachel hadn't retreated emotionally when they woke up, which he'd half expected her to do.

He'd dropped her off at the main house, leaving her with the promise to return with the signed warrant. And he aimed to keep that promise.

Parking outside the church, Adam entered through a side door and scanned the room filled with the aroma of maple syrup and bacon. The judge and several other men sat at a table against the far wall, close to another side door. Perfect.

Threading his way between tables, he exchanged

greetings as they came his way, keeping them short but friendly.

He stopped next to the judge, addressing his dining companions. "Good morning, Mayor, Councilmen." He offered a quick tip of his hat. "Judge Harmon, could I speak with you about an urgent matter? It'll only take a few moments of your time."

Harmon exchanged a glance with the mayor, laid his knife and fork on his plate and sighed. "Deputy Reed, I'm trying to enjoy my breakfast here. Surely this can wait for Monday morning."

"Sorry, Your Honor, but it can't. It's a matter of life and death."

The judge slapped his paper napkin on the table, stood and followed Adam out the side door.

"What life-and-death matter are you talking about?"

"This warrant request has to do with the recent murders we've had and a threat of cartel and gang violence in Boone County." Adam held the papers out toward the judge. "We could be too late if we can't search this storage unit immediately."

"That so?" Harmon retrieved his reading glasses from his pocket and settled them on his nose, then reached for the affidavit with an arthritic hand speckled with age spots. "I'll tell you, son, I'm appalled at the growing crime in our county. Weren't near this bad when your daddy was sheriff."

"Yes, sir." This particular conversation occurred several times a month, if not with Adam, then with Cassie. Agreeing with the old man always proved to be the fastest way to get what they wanted.

Adam waited patiently while the judge read the entire affidavit. After he had Adam swear the information was correct, Harmon signed the warrant and handed it back. “Don’t screw it up.”

“No, sir.” Adam speed-walked back to his truck. He had no intention of screwing up anything with this case.

Chapter Fifteen

"Did he sign it?" Rachel asked, the second Adam walked in the door.

"He signed it. Wasn't too happy about being separated from his breakfast for a few minutes, but he wants this case solved, and fast."

Noah and Bree rose from the couch.

"We're going with you," Noah said, his arm around Bree's shoulders.

"Me, too."

The three deputies looked at Rachel.

"I think it would be better—" Adam started.

"Oh no, you don't. I'm the one in danger from this guy. I'm coming along." Her chin jutted out. "Besides, being with three deputies is a whole lot safer than me being here by myself."

"Nate's upstairs." Noah cringed from the glare Rachel turned on him.

Adam gave in. "Fine, you can come."

They took Adam's truck. Rachel called shotgun; Noah and Bree sat in the back seat.

As they drove northwest on Highway 111, Rachel

angled her position so she could see Adam's profile without being obvious. "Isn't Hudsonville where Cassie and Bishop went after those human traffickers last summer?" The crime had been so horrific, even the talking heads on cable news had featured it.

"Yep. Sure am glad that case is in the rearview mirror." Adam glanced at her. "What?"

"Nothing. I'm just taking in the scenery." She slid her line of sight past him to the side window, but his smirk made it obvious he'd caught her watching him.

He turned off the highway well before Hudsonville and took a back road northeast.

"We there already?" Noah asked.

Adam glanced in his side mirror. "No. I'm making sure we aren't being tailed."

Rachel whipped around in her seat to look out the back window, surprised to find Noah and Bree paying no attention to the possible danger.

"Relax. There's no one behind us right now. But we're going to take the long way just to be safe." Adam took a left turn and continued to zigzag his way north. Twice, he pulled to the side of the road and waited a few minutes before continuing.

Relieved when Adam finally pulled to a stop in front of Vic's Self Storage, Rachel unbuckled her seat belt and jumped out. He and the others joined her, walking toward the house next door where the owner lived. At least, that's what the sign said.

"Not trying to be rude here, but let me do *all* the talking, okay?" Adam glanced at Noah and Bree, then focused on Rachel. "You're not law enforcement, and while he can think you are, you can't claim to be."

"I get the impression you *want* him to assume I'm a cop."

"We don't usually take civilians along when we serve search warrants," Adam said.

"Got it, Chief Deputy Reed, sir." She smiled up at him, and he laughed.

Adam knocked on the front door, and it swung open. A scowling middle-aged man said, "Yeah?"

"Are you Hank?" When the man nodded, Adam handed him the search warrant.

He glanced over it. "I'll buzz you through the front gate. Turn right, then take the third left. Eighty-six is toward the far end." His eyes roamed across Rachel in a hungry way that she didn't appreciate, but she held her tongue. "Gate'll open automatically on your way out."

Adam drove slowly down the aisle, and they all strained to read the unit numbers.

"Eighty-six." Rachel pointed up ahead to the left.

In case the unit didn't have an interior light, Adam parked so the truck's headlights could shine in that direction. Adam, Noah and Bree pulled on gloves, and he handed Rachel a pair. "Don't touch anything without wearing gloves. Trying to explain how your prints or DNA got in there would be tricky."

Crouching by the lock, he examined it. "Same brand as the key. And it's a discus lock. Eric bought himself a good one."

"This is like digging for buried treasure." Rachel's stomach flip-flopped. "Hurry."

He unlocked the padlock and set it on the ground.

Noah pulled up the unit's door, and inside sat a white cargo van. Rachel followed Adam along the side of it, observing small holes in the vehicle, more as they approached the driver's door.

After inspecting those, Adam rounded the front and let out a low whistle. "Look." He pointed at the windshield, riddled with circular cracks that looked like small targets. "This is an armored van. Those are mushroomed bullets that didn't pierce all the layers of laminated glass."

"I've never seen what happens to a bullet when it hits a windshield like this." Noah leaned in for a closer look.

"But I saw bullet holes in the side panels." Rachel walked back to look at them again. "And why are the doors black, like they were burned?"

"I'd bet that's how Eric and Smith got the gang members out of the van. If they held flamethrowers or something similar against the doors, it would heat up the inside. They'd either have to get out or risk getting cooked." Opening the driver's door, Adam showed her there were no holes on the inside. "The armoring is inside the exterior panels. Each layer dissipates the bullet's energy."

After finding the ignition key under the front floor mat, and the inside lever to unlock the rear doors, Adam joined Rachel at the back of the van. They pulled the doors open, and Rachel spread her arms wide. "Hallelujah."

Medium-sized shipping boxes, taped shut, lay in a haphazard mess between two bench seats. A *lot* of boxes. Two near the door had been opened, and now Adam pushed the top flaps aside so they could see the contents. Money. Lots of money, all in bundles.

Bree picked one up and tapped the plain white currency strap. "This is what I found at your apartment."

"If Eric had the van and money, how did his partner have some of the bands?" Rachel had never seen as much money as a single bundle held.

"The Victoria detective I spoke with said there were some blood-stained bands on the ground at the crime scene. Maybe some fell out during the hijacking and Smith grabbed what he could." He scanned the van's interior. "Looks like room for two or three gang members on each bench."

Rachel walked outside, lowered the tailgate on Adam's truck and sat on it. "What happens next?"

"We wait here while I coordinate between our department and the Victoria police, maybe the Victoria County Sheriff. The hijacking of the van may not have been within the city limits. Whoever claims it will have it towed to their impound lot or forensics center." Adam sat next to her.

"You'll have them meet you here today?"

"Right. I need a signed receipt from them for the van and the money." Adam shook his head. "Sure glad I don't have to deal with moving the money anywhere myself."

"How will the hitman find out his money's been seized?" She eagerly anticipated that part. Rachel already felt the weight of the past weeks floating away. "He'll go back to Mexico once he knows, right?"

"I'll ask Solis to have his department, their sheriff's office, or maybe both, send out a news alert to the papers and news stations. See if he can get it on the national news and in some bigger papers than just the one in Victoria. I'll ask him to leave Boone County, you and me out of the story." He caught her looking at him again. "What?"

"You didn't mention the bad guy leaving the country."

He rubbed the back of his neck, and Rachel prepared herself for whatever he was about to say, because it wouldn't be good.

"Thing is, I still need to go after him for Smith's murder. *That* happened in *my* county."

Rachel folded her arms across her chest, her mood not quite as joyous anymore. Adam was working on keeping her out of harm's way. It hurt her heart to think he planned on stepping right back into its path.

RACHEL AND ADAM sat on his tailgate while he jotted down notes. He'd claimed he wanted his ducks lined up before he called Victoria PD. Noah and Bree loitered at the back of the van, trying to guess how much money was in it.

When Rachel's phone rang, she glanced at the screen. "It's my mom. I didn't call her yesterday. She must be worried sick." She answered the call. "Hi, Mom. I'm sor—"

Her hand reached blindly for Adam's arm, and when

she found it, she squeezed, her nails biting into his flesh. She clicked the phone's Mute button and said, "Don't make a sound." When he nodded, she put her phone on Speaker.

"Understand?" a deep male voice asked.

She unmuted the phone. "Sorry, I'm on my way to work, and I had to pull over. I didn't hear what you said." Her entire body had begun to shake, and she barely noticed Noah and Bree edging closer.

The male voice cursed, then repeated his words. "I am with your family. Your mother, children, aunt. Do you hear me now?"

"Yes." Rachel's voice came out as a whisper.

"I am not in the habit of hurting children and old women—"

"Who are you calling old, you disgusting hooligan?" Several *thwap*s sounded after Aunt Sylvie's question.

"Lady, if you don't sit down and shut up, I'll only have one old woman to deal with."

Thwap.

"Stop hitting me with that pillow," the man said. A low grunt, a high-pitched gasp, then silence.

"What did you do to my aunt?" Rachel pictured Aunt Sylvie's body on the floor.

"Nothing. I took the damn couch pillow away from her. As I was saying, I don't *usually* hurt innocent kids and women. But if you don't bring me the money your husband stole, I will have to. One by one. Slowly. Painfully."

"I don't know where the money is. Eric and I were divorced—"

"And Smith's trail led to you. Which means Eric told him you have it. Listen carefully. I know you're staying with the Reeds, so you must need protection. Don't tell your deputy boyfriend about this call. Don't tell anyone. Just come alone with the money to your aunt's house, and everyone will live happily ever after."

"How do I know you'll let them go?" Rachel avoided looking at Adam, afraid one compassionate glance from him would shatter her resolve. "I want to talk to my mom. Make sure she's alive."

Martina's voice sounded like it came from across a room. "I'm okay, honey. We're all okay. I'm sorry, this—"

"Satisfied?"

"At least let my kids go. They can't—"

"They all stay. Now, stop talking, get the money and bring it to me. Your deadline is midnight tonight." In the background, Daisy began to cry. "Don't try anything. If anyone other than you shows up, no one will leave here alive." The call ended.

Now she met Adam's eyes, hers already filling with tears.

Adam put his arms around her. "Don't cry, Rach. I'll take care of this."

She'd hated when Eric called her Rach. But when it came from Adam, she welcomed it as an endearment. "How?" The waver in her voice caught her off guard.

"I'll call the San Antonio police. They've got a big department. They can get a SWAT team ready, and Noah and I'll head up there, lights and sirens screaming."

Rachel placed her hands on Adam's chest and

pushed him away from her. "Absolutely not! You just heard him. If he sees any cops, deputies, *anyone*, he'll kill my babies. My mom."

"There's nothing else we can do. You certainly can't go up there alone and face off with him." He looked at her as if he thought *she* was the crazy one.

"Oh yes, I can." She narrowed her eyes and held out her open palm. "Give me the keys to the van."

STUNNED, ADAM JUST sat there. He'd watched the blood drain from her face less than five minutes ago, and now she glared at him, flushed with intent. That it happened to be criminal intent didn't escape him. But she wasn't acting out of personal greed. To be honest, her willingness to go to any lengths to save her family impressed him. But still…

"That money isn't ours. I have to turn it in." He looked to Noah and Bree, expecting support. Instead, they avoided his eyes.

"Why? It's money from illegal activities. It belonged to a gang who planned to give it to a cartel. It doesn't belong to the Victoria police or the Victoria County Sheriff or anyone else." Rachel's voice took on a hard edge. "We're the ones who found it. If it wasn't for you, no one would know where it is. No one *does* know where it is. Not for sure. You can just say the van wasn't in the storage locker."

Adam rubbed a spot over his left eye, where a headache started to pound. "Rachel, listen to me. If you drive that van to San Antonio, anything could happen. It could break down. This guy might have associates watching the route. They could run you off the road, kill you and steal the money."

"It's an armored van, Adam. All I'd have to do is keep the doors closed."

"Your ex managed to empty that van by heating it up like a pouch of microwave popcorn. If it worked for him, it could work for the bad guys if they manage to stop you in it."

"You know what I'm hearing? *Might* and *could.* But you know what's for sure? My family being killed if I don't do this. It's the only way I can save them."

"And what's to stop him from killing all of you as soon as you hand him the key to the van? Why would he let any of you go?"

"Then, come with me. Help me." Her voice broke.

Adam blew out a frustrated breath, but he brought his tone down. "Do you realize what you're asking me to do? I've got a warrant from the judge to search for the van and money. I located it. The guy who owns the storage place knows I've been here. If I drive out of here in the van, he'll have security footage of it. I'd be taking something that should be put into evidence and handing it over to a cartel hitman. You're asking me to break the law. To thumb my nose at my job. To lose my career and possibly go to prison."

"I'm asking you to help me save my family." She looked at him from beneath glistening lashes. "What would you do if it were your family? If someone had a gun to Cassie's head, Noah's or Nate's? Would you put *anything* ahead of their lives?"

She wanted him to do something that went against

every lawful bone in his body, that denied the ideals ingrained in him since he was a child. But what Rachel said hit a nerve. *Nothing* would stop him from saving one of his siblings.

He pictured Brad's giggling face as he held up his baseball bear, Daisy dropping her binky in Rachel's lap, Martina showing him more maternal affection than his own mom had during Adam's first ten years. He couldn't, he wouldn't, let anything happen to them.

He took hold of Rachel's hand. "Okay. I'll help. No cops, no SWAT."

She threw her arms around his neck and hugged him. "Thank you."

"How do you want do this?" Noah asked. "Bree and I can—"

"No." Adam had to shut this down now. "You two just heard our whole conversation. I'm not letting either one of you risk your careers or get arrested."

"Adam," Bree said. "You can't do this by yourself. You have to have backup."

"I'm not budging on this. If you and Noah don't agree to turn around and go back to Resolute, this idea is dead in the water." Adam appreciated them more than he could say, but he wouldn't let them get involved in this. And he'd play dirty if he had to. "And if that's the case, you can both tell Rachel how sorry you are for—"

"All right, all right. We'll go home on one condition." Noah waited for Adam to ask what it was. When he didn't, he continued. "Take Nate with you."

Although not eager to put either of his brothers in

harm's way, Adam had to admit that Nate *would* be a good alternative. He wasn't in law enforcement, so he wouldn't lose his job and Adam could probably keep him out of jail. Plus, he had skills from being a body-guard that might come in handy.

Talking about skills, too bad Bishop was out of town. Teamed with Adam and Nate, the private investigator would've been the perfect backup.

"Fine. You two drive my truck back to the ranch, and I'll call Nate. But I'm letting him decide for himself whether or not he wants to come."

"Deal." Bree hugged Rachel. "Don't take any chances."

Rachel nodded. "Thanks for offering. But I'm glad you're staying out of it."

Before his truck disappeared from sight, Adam was on the phone to Nate. "I need your help. But first I have to tell you what's happening, so you can say no if you want."

After Adam explained everything, Nate said, "Dude."

"I know." Adam sighed, waiting for his younger brother's answer.

"Hell, yeah, I'm coming. Let me change and grab some guns."

Chapter Sixteen

Ten minutes after Nate drove into the storage facility in his truck he drove back out, Adam following with Rachel in the van. They could have been out of there in five if Nate hadn't insisted on seeing the money while they were still safely hidden away.

They made the two-hour drive mostly in silence, Adam preoccupied by figuring out how they were going to pull this off.

Rachel seemed to be off in her own world, staring out the side window. Then out of the blue, she turned to him and said, "Can I ask you something?"

"Sure." He expected a question about their mission. What they each were looking at for possible jail time if they were caught, or how they'd handle the hitman if he really did intend to kill them all.

"The first day I stayed at your ranch, why did you get depressed when I mentioned that cabin near the house? Why is it off-limits?"

It took him a minute to comprehend what she'd said, it was so unexpected. "It was my mom's art studio. My dad put a lock on the door the day after she left, and it's been locked ever since." He glanced at her. "Well, that's not entirely true. I found out last year that Cassie had gone into it when she moved to her house. She took Mom's pottery wheel and some other art supplies. She's the only artistic one in the family. I mean, besides Mom."

"I'm sorry I upset you that day. I had no idea."

"No way you could have. That building holds a lot of our emotions hostage. It was where Mom spent most of her time, so it represented her. But it was why she and Dad argued so much. Mom neglected everything, everyone, to focus on her art. Dad felt like the cabin was competing with him for his wife's attention."

"That must have been horrible."

"When I found out about Cassie going in there behind Dad's back, I was angry. I had no idea she'd been so afraid of turning out like our mom she'd been trying to deny her artistic ability." He met Rachel's compassion-filled eyes and smiled. "She's so talented."

"Thanks for telling me. It's been bothering me that I caused distress as soon as I'd arrived."

"Don't give it another thought. I haven't."

As they approached the neighborhood where her aunt lived, Nate called Adam.

"There's a grocery store three blocks up, on the left." Before they left the storage facility, Nate had plugged in Sylvie's address and pulled up street and satellite views of the one-story residence. He'd apparently done a little more reconnaissance at the same time. "Pull in there while I make a pass on the aunt's street and the one behind it. I'll call you when I find a good place to park my truck, and you come pick me up."

A short while later, Adam's cell rang. "I'm two streets north of the target. Pick me up on the west cross street."

"Got it."

Once Nate was in the van, Adam drove back to the grocery store. He wanted to avoid parking in the neighborhood until it was time. He knew all too well how some people liked to report unfamiliar vehicles parked in front of their house.

Nate filled them in. "Her next-door neighbor's side fence starts about five yards farther back than the aunt's does."

"Her name is Sylvie," Rachel said.

"Okay." Nate acknowledged the input. "So we can hop Sylvie's side fence, then work our way around to the back. I'm just not sure how we'll get inside from there."

"He'll probably have all the doors locked." Adam looked at his brother. "Garage, maybe?"

"Rachel, how many doors in Sylvie's house?" Nate was pulling the views back up on his iPad.

"Front door, back sliding glass door in the living room, back door in the kitchen and an inside door to the garage."

"He might not have locked the garage door." Nate looked up from his tablet.

"Aunt Sylvie always keeps all the doors locked, even when she's home."

"Great." Adam sighed. "She doesn't have an alarm system, does she?"

Rachel shook her head. "Why don't you just use the key and go in through the kitchen door? If they're still in the living room, it would be hard to hear it open from there."

"Key?" Adam and Nate looked at each other, then both turned to Rachel. "You have a key?"

"No, but there's one in the fake rock out back near the kitchen. It unlocks all the doors except the sliding glass." When they kept looking at her, she said, "Sorry. I'm a little distracted."

"No problem. That solves that." Nate smiled.

"Rachel's going to have to be the one to knock on the front door. He can't know you and I are anywhere near San Antonio." And Adam didn't want *her* anywhere near the killer. He'd never forgive himself if something happened to her.

"I brought an extra gun, if you think you can handle one." Nate eyed Rachel.

"Absolutely not," Adam said, furious. "What if he searches her?"

"He won't find this one, bro." Nate leaned forward from the jump seat behind Rachel. "You're wearing boots, right?"

She nodded, pulling one foot up in an awkward position so he could see her Western boot.

Nate passed Adam a short-barrel derringer in a small ankle holster. Adam took the gun from the holster and held it up between his fingers. "This peashooter?" he scoffed.

"It's better than no weapon at all."

Adam rolled his eyes. "Turn sideways and put your

right foot up here." He patted his knee. With her boot on his leg, he tugged it off and strapped the holster just above her ankle bone.

Nate spoke to Rachel. "When you go inside, he'll be holding his gun. Try to shy away from it, act scared. If you get a chance, say something about being afraid of guns. He may not search you at all if he believes you."

Showing the gun to Rachel, Adam instructed her on its use. "Its range is maybe a little farther than five yards, but only for a very accurate shooter. If you have to use it, try to be as close as possible so that he's a bigger target." He met her eyes, and instead of the fearful expression he'd expected, she looked determined. He tucked the gun into the holster and held her boot while she pushed her foot in.

"Let's go save my family."

RACHEL DROPPED ADAM and Nate at the end of the block, then continued along the side street. The plan was for her to stall until they figured out their best move. Two blocks down, her phone chirped and she answered. Adam's voice came over the speaker in a whisper.

"We've got the key. The living-room curtains are open, and I peeked in from the patio-door edge. He's got your family together on the couch, and he's in a chair across from them but facing away from the backyard. Can he see the front door from that room?"

"No. The hallway wall blocks it. He has to go down the long hall, then turn right into the foyer."

"Okay, good. When you park in front, text me before you turn off the truck. Instead of knocking, ring the bell so we hear it. When he goes to the door, we'll come in through the kitchen."

"All right."

"Rachel? Be careful."

"I will. You, too."

"I love you."

Her breath caught in her throat. Her heart wanted to take flight, like a butterfly or hummingbird. But it didn't stand a chance against the pressure filling her chest. Were Adam's words a harbinger of happiness to come? Or a dark omen, jinxing what they were about to attempt?

She made her way back to Aunt Sylvie's and pulled to the curb. Keeping her phone on her knee, she texted Here to Adam, turned off the motor and climbed out of the van before she lost her nerve. As she walked up the front path, she summoned every ounce of strength and resolve she knew she possessed and held on to it as she pressed the doorbell.

When the door swung in, a man faced her, one arm wrapped around her mother's midriff, the other holding a gun to her mother's head.

"Mom." Rachel took a step toward her, but the man shook his head.

He stepped back. "Come in and close the door."

She did as instructed, willing herself to stay calm. Focused. "Are you okay, Mom?"

Martina gave a quick nod before the man waved his gun toward the hallway. "To the living room."

Rachel let out a small squeak, wrapped her arms

around herself and backed up. "P-p-please don't swing your gun like that. I'm already scared enough."

"Move." He pointed the gun at Rachel.

When she stepped into the living room, Brad jumped up and ran to her.

"Mommy! Mommy! Mommy!" He threw himself against her legs and clamped on for dear life.

Smoothing his hair, she crouched in front of him. "Are you okay, baby?"

He nodded. "We get pizza now. Joe says we get pizza."

"You do?" Rachel looked to Sylvie, holding the baby out in front of her about a foot above her lap. "Everything all right, Aunt Sylvie?"

"I think this one needs to be changed." She wrinkled her nose.

Rachel stood and faced the man with the gun. "Joe, huh?" Nice, mundane choice for a killer.

He shrugged. "Works as well as any other name." He released Martina, who took Daisy from Sylvie.

"I need to change her." Martina shot a nervous glance toward the man as she laid Daisy on a baby blanket on the floor, grabbed a diaper from the coffee table and got to work.

"Brad, honey, why don't you go help Meemaw change your sister's diaper?" Terrified her son would get hurt if he stayed near her, she walked him over to her mother.

Signaling Rachel to join him in the middle of the room, Joe made an announcement. "We—" he held Rachel as he'd been holding Martina "—are going to step outside for a moment. You've all been very cooperative today. Continue that for a few more minutes, and this will all be over. But if you try anything, she—" he placed the muzzle of his gun against Rachel's ear "—will be the first to go."

THE MOMENT THE front door closed, Adam ran to the living room, Nate right on his heels. Rachel's aunt cowered on the couch, her lips opening wide to scream. Nate managed to get his hand over her mouth in time to muffle it.

With the baby in her arms, Martina rushed to Adam. "Thank God you're here." She glanced at her sister. "Sylvie, stop it. They're here to rescue us."

Nate helped Sylvie to stand, then unlocked and opened the patio door.

"We have to go right now." Adam picked up Brad and put a hand on Martina's back, urging her out the door.

Once on the patio, Nate took Sylvie's arm and guided her to the far side of the house, where the fence had a gate. Martina, still carrying Daisy, stayed right behind them. After closing the back door but not locking it, Adam caught up to them.

"No one make a sound," Nate whispered as he swung the gate open. "Keep close."

They flattened themselves against the side of the next-door neighbor's house and eased forward until Nate held up his hand. He held the group there while Adam set Brad on his feet, had Martina take the boy's hand and then dashed across the side yard to Sylvie's house and inched his way toward the front.

The gunman stood right behind Rachel with an arm around her waist, facing the house. Adam could just make out the gun pressed against Rachel's back.

She dug her heels into the sidewalk, forcing him to stop, and her angry voice carried in the still air. "Why don't you just take the money right now and go?"

Rachel was smart, and Adam realized she knew there was only one reason for the killer to go back inside. Take care of the witnesses. Urgency flowed through Adam, his arms tingling with it. Once this hit-man learned everyone else had escaped, Rachel was living on borrowed time.

"Move now or I'll drag you the rest of the way." He shoved her forward, never releasing his grip on her or the gun.

Adam raced back to the group. "They're inside. Let's go." He herded Martina and Brad around the corner while Nate grabbed Sylvie's arm and rushed her forward a few steps.

Nate would get them inside the neighbor's house for safekeeping while Adam sneaked into Sylvie's through the front door and confronted the assassin. Meanwhile, Nate would sneak back in through the now-unlocked patio door and they'd have him surrounded as best they could.

Adam, halfway across Sylvie's front lawn, turned at an abruptly ended shriek. Dropping into a crouch next to some large bushes for cover, he looked back.

Sylvie had apparently tripped over something and face-planted in the neighbor's yard. Nate hurried to help her up as Daisy started crying. When Martina let go of Brad's hand to quiet the baby, the boy took off running toward Adam, calling for his mother.

Adam hesitated only a moment before running to intercept Brad, but Nate wasn't taking any chances. He let go of Sylvie, now on her knees, and hightailed it to grab the boy. Sylvie surrendered to gravity upon Nate's release and, leading with her nose, replanted herself.

Grabbing Brad, Nate waved for his brother to keep going. Adam raced to the front door and turned the knob, saying a silent prayer of gratitude when it turned and the door swung in without a sound.

AS THEY ROUNDED the hall corner, Joe froze, his hold on Rachel tightening like a boa constrictor. His gun went to her ear.

The living room was empty. As scared as she was for herself, Rachel's relief that her children were safe was tenfold.

"Get back in here or she's dead!" his voice thundered throughout the house. With his gun still against her ear, he pulled zip ties from his pocket and made Rachel cuff her hands in front of herself.

"Let her go." Adam's voice, quiet, carried a vindictive chill.

Joe spun at the sound, putting Rachel between himself and Adam. The barrel of his gun pushed farther into her ear, pressing her head sideways. He *tsk*ed three times. "I told you not to bring anyone with you, didn't I?"

Adam blocked the path to the front door. "You'll never make it out of here."

One second the iron gunsight drilled into her ear canal, the next it was gone. Her head lifted of its own accord, and she opened her eyes to find the gun now pointed at Adam. The two men stood as if in an old-time duel that neither would win.

"No! Adam, stop. Let him leave with the money." None of this was worth a pile of dirty cash.

"He plans on taking you with him. I'm not letting that happen."

The gun barrel was back in her ear before Rachel knew it.

"Back away, or I *will* kill her."

The pressure against her ear, almost unbearable now, brought tears to her eyes. Her captor kept his back to the patio, using her as his shield. There was no way Adam could hit him without hitting her, too.

Adam must have realized the same thing, because he began to back down the long hallway. Joe moved toward the foyer, always keeping Rachel in Adam's line of fire. Sidestepping to the door, his gun now trained on Adam, Joe said, "Turn the knob and pull it open."

The moment Rachel did, Adam rushed toward the foyer, and Joe fired at him. Rachel screamed as he fell back in the hallway, only his boots visible from where she stood. The killer tightened his grip and lifted her against him, her feet dangling inches above the ground as he ran for the van.

Nate raced from the side of the house, his gun raised, but the killer dragged her to the street side of the van and threw her into the front seat.

Rachel scrambled over the center console and

yanked on the door handle. *Locked.* Same story with the window. Her fingers slid across the panel, unable to find a button to unlock either one. She pounded on the passenger window. "He killed Adam!" she yelled, choking on tears and heartbreak. As the van pulled away, she witnessed Nate's anguished expression a second before he turned and ran for the house.

He killed Adam.

Chapter Seventeen

Adam lay on the hallway floor, unable to move but taking stock. His Kevlar vest saved his life, and for that he was thankful. But even with the armored plates, the bullet had done plenty of damage to his chest. He'd worry about that later. Right now his only concern was Rachel.

The front door slammed open, and Nate skidded to a stop next to him. He dropped to his knees, tears rolling down his face.

"Took you long enough. Some backup you are." Every few words were punctuated with a wheeze. "Help me up. We've got to follow them."

Nate dropped back on his haunches. "You're not dead? Rachel said you were dead." Nate pulled at the vest's Velcro straps and lifted it. "I don't see any blood. You sure you're okay?"

"I'm fine. Get the truck."

"I'll go after her." Nate helped Adam stand. "You'll just slow me down." He raced out of the house before Adam could argue.

Frustration welled. He'd promised to keep Rachel safe. *He* had promised. Adam took a step toward the front door, gasped in pain and grabbed the wall. He sucked in air between gritted teeth as sweat dripped past his eyes. He'd narrowly avoided passing out while Nate got him up on his feet. Cracked ribs, no doubt. But the shock to his entire body from the bullet's kinetic energy took him by surprise.

Keeping one hand on the wall, he shuffled toward the front door. The stillness of the house bothered him. Her family was safe, which eased his heart. But Rachel wasn't. Their plan should have worked, damn it. Instead, Nate had been late, Adam had been shot, and Rachel had been taken hostage.

Rachel thinks I'm dead. His pulse began to race. Surely, she wouldn't do anything reckless because of that. She wouldn't put revenge above her own safety. She had two kids to take care of, a mother who loved her. Even if his vest had failed and he *had* died, his death couldn't mean as much to Rachel as her family.

CURLED UP IN the passenger seat, Rachel stared at the monster who had murdered Adam. Her love. Her life. Her future. She wanted to spring across the console, dig her thumbs into his eye sockets, slam his head against the glass strong enough to stop bullets. Instead, she waited.

He glanced sideways at her. "Sit straight and fasten your seat belt. I'm not going to get stopped because you didn't buckle up."

She sat up in her seat, put her feet on the floor. It took two tries to get the seat belt clicked in. "So where are we going now?" She rested her bound hands in her lap.

Joe barked out a laugh. "That's nothing you need to know."

"And you obviously don't need me." She refused to beg. At least, for now. "Why don't you let me out, and you can ride away into the sunset with your money."

The man continued to laugh, aggravating Rachel.

"You're not a run-of-the-mill hitman, are you?" She tipped her head, studying him like a bug under a microscope. "You said you didn't like to kill children and old women. I bet you never intended to hurt anyone in my family, did you?"

He stopped at a red light, looking through the windshield at cars zipping crosswise in front of them. "I do what I am hired to do. By whatever means necessary."

"So you would have murdered a baby? A five-year-old boy?"

The light changed, and he drove through the busy intersection without saying a word. Either he didn't want to admit he would have hurt her children or he didn't like repeating himself. Most likely the latter. Rachel doubted the man had a compassionate bone in his body.

"You still haven't said why you won't let me go."

They turned off the main boulevard and onto a residential street. He braked at a stop sign, and while he waited for a woman with a little girl to cross the street, he turned his head toward Rachel. The anger in his expression made a strong counterpoint to the laughter of children playing in the park next to them.

"Instead of following my instructions, you brought others with you. Actions have consequences."

Now was the time to beg. As he drove on, Rachel sniffled. She sobbed, thinking of what might have happened to Brad and Daisy. To her mother. And she folded in half with grief. Adam was dead. Because of her. She had asked him to help her, and he had, but it had cost him his life.

And when they approached a red light at a quiet intersection, with no other vehicles, no pedestrians, no children at play, she leaned toward him, and before he could turn his head, she shoved her derringer in his right ear and pulled the trigger.

THE BLARE OF multiple sirens shook Adam from his musings. They were close, and he still didn't believe in coincidences. Had the killer tossed Rachel's body from the van when he no longer needed her as a hostage? That and numerous other scenarios rolled through his mind, each one worse than the last. An excruciating pain in his chest that had nothing to do with broken ribs almost brought him to his knees. He didn't want to consider a life without Rachel Miller in it.

When Nate's truck bounced against the front curb and Rachel jumped out, Adam made his way down the front walk, joy numbing his physical aches.

She dashed toward him, her arms opening for a hug. "You're alive!"

Adam held both of his hands out in a gesture to halt, cringing at the hurt look that spread across her face.

She pulled up short in front of him, her face wet with tears that still flowed.

His own eyes dampened at the sight of her. He spread his arms slightly in welcome, wheezing with each breath. "Come here. Just don't hug me."

She came forward, one slow step at a time. "Can I kiss you? Or do your lips hurt, too?"

Adam patted the fingers of one hand against his lips. "Nope, lips don't seem to hurt. Let's give it a shot."

By the time they pulled apart, they were surrounded by Rachel's family, who Nate had retrieved from next door.

Martina came in like a wrecking ball to hug Adam, but Rachel ran interference and blocked her.

"I want pizza!" Brad jumped up and down. "I want pizza!"

Daisy, with the bewildered look of someone who'd just woken from a nap, started crying in Sylvie's arms. Sylvie handed the baby to Nate, shook her head at the commotion and went inside.

Adam caught Nate's eye over Rachel's head and raised his brows. Nate pointed at Rachel, then made a finger gun and pointed it at his own head. Relieved that the kidnapper was dead, Adam mentally prepared himself for what Rachel would be going through. Taking a life was never easy, even when that life belonged to a death-dealing mercenary without a soul.

SHE KILLED A MAN.

Rachel waited. For guilt to start eating at her. For regret to fill her heart. For shame to destroy her inner strength.

They had left her mom and kids at Aunt Sylvie's for now, and for the entire drive from San Antonio back to Resolute in Nate's truck, she waited.

But by the time she, Adam and Nate arrived at the ranch that evening, it had become obvious she didn't need to wait any longer. The death of a heinous assassin at her hands would never torture her conscience. Especially after he'd threatened her children and held a gun to her mom's head.

When they walked into the house, Noah welcomed them with nonstop questions, despite Nate calling on the way home with the highlights.

Adam lowered himself onto the couch in slow motion, and Rachel sat next to him.

"What's it feel like to get hit in the vest?" Noah asked.

Bree punched his arm. "Seriously?"

"Sort of like a sledgehammer hit to the solar plexus, if Paul Bunyan were doing the swinging." Since the EMTs had wrapped his rib cage for him, Adam's wheezing had improved. But they'd still made him promise to get X-rays when he got home.

Bree, quiet for much of the conversation, kept flicking glances at Rachel, who finally said, "I'm fine."

"That's not… But if you ever need to talk…" A shooting incident when Bree was a San Antonio cop had had an indelible effect on her, leaving her with an empathy for that type of PTSD.

Rachel smiled. "Thanks. I appreciate that." But she would never take her friend up on the offer. Shooting Joe would *not* be taking up space in her head or in her heart.

Adam Reed, however, was a completely different space-taker-upper.

As if reading her mind, Adam leaned over as best he could. “Can we step outside?” he whispered. “I need a little air.”

When Rachel stood, Nate helped pull Adam to his feet. “Think you better stick to hard chairs for a while, dude, so you don’t sink into the cushions.”

Rachel followed Adam out to the back patio, and they strolled through the yard. Neither spoke, but this silence wasn’t that awkward type she’d hated during their short friend-zone period. This was comfortable, easy.

Shoulder to shoulder, arms occasionally touching, they passed the fragrant plantings she’d enjoyed the night of their first kiss. His hand took hold of hers, and their fingers intertwined, Rachel’s pulse quickening with just that simple touch.

Adam stopped when they reached the orange tree. Turning toward her, he took hold of her other hand, too, and a sudden warmth swept through her. Overwhelmed with his romantic gesture, she readied herself for another kiss. Whether an encore or a do-over, just that he chose the same setting was enough to make her heart expand.

“This has been one hell of a day, and it probably isn’t the best time for this. But I’m afraid if I don’t say this now, I’ll lose my nerve.” He held her hands against his palms now, trapped by his thumbs. “I’ve had feelings for you since we were kids. You probably found some of that out over the past few weeks. And I meant what I said in San Antonio. I love you."

Those three words sat poised on Rachel's tongue, too, waiting for the perfect moment to tell Adam he'd captured her heart *and* her mind. There would be no more battles between the two.

"I also know you've been working your butt off to get a degree, and you already have plans for it. Job offers in other cities. Better opportunities for you and your kids." He let go of one of her hands and rubbed the back of his neck.

And just like that, she knew Adam Reed was about to shatter her fantasy.

"This is probably the last thing I ever thought I'd say to you, but I don't want to come between you and the life you've been dreaming of. I love you too much to ask you to stay in Resolute. You already gave up your dreams once when you married Eric, and even though you came out of it with the two greatest kids in the world, it's not fair of me to ask you to do it again." His voice thickened with emotion, and the full moon's light revealed tears in his eyes.

Her heart now slamming against her ribs, Rachel inhaled a shaky breath. She'd had the strength to end the life of one man today. Surely, she had enough left to open her heart to another.

"I love *you*, Adam. I love your kindness, your gentleness, your generosity. The way you are with my kids, as well as my mom." She let go of his hand and reached up, laying her palms against his cheeks. "Loving you, staying in Resolute to be with you, wouldn't be giving up my dreams. It would be fulfilling them."

She went up on her tiptoes and gave him a gentle kiss. Adam's hands cupped the back of her head, returning the kiss and then some.

Rachel especially liked the then some.

When they finally stopped for air, Adam's mouth curved into a sheepish smile. "I didn't want to jinx anything, so I don't have a ring to give you."

She raised one brow. "You've got some time to shop. I'm not accepting a ring until you can get down on one knee and ask me all properlike. *And* get up again by yourself. But I do have one serious question I need an answer to first."

His smile faded, and he raised a brow.

"Exactly how many more kids are we talking about? I looked it up, but the definition for *passel* doesn't give a specific number."

"I thought you said you didn't want any more." The thread of excitement in his voice made her all the more confident in her decision.

"That was before I knew what a fantastic father you'll be."

He wrapped his arms around her lightly and kissed her again.

Just then the patio door opened.

"You've got to be kidding," he mumbled against her lips.

They turned to see the others standing in the doorway with big grins on their faces.

"Congratulations!" Noah yelled. "Now, get in here. I found a peach pie in the freezer."

Epilogue

Three months later

With Daisy on one hip and holding Brad's hand, Rachel wove her way through the crowd gathering in front of the new Boone County Youth Center. The air, scented with smoked brisket and grilled burgers, crackled with excitement. The day had finally arrived for the ribbon-cutting ceremony.

"Have you seen Adam?" she asked Noah, who was trying to eat a brisket sandwich without dripping barbecue sauce on his shirt.

"I saw him a little while ago, talking to Cassie." He turned in a circle, looking over heads for another tall Reed brother. "There they are." Noah pointed toward the parking lot.

"Thanks." She took one step, then was brought up short by a five-year-old anchor.

"I want a hamburger, Mommy." Brad yanked on her arm. "I'm hungry."

"Go on." Noah took Brad's hand from Rachel's. "Little dude and I are going to get us some food. Right?"

"Right!" Brad yelled. "Hamburger."

"But…I…" Rachel said.

"Don't worry, I won't lose him." Noah looked at Brad and turned him around in a circle. "Wait, where's his leash?"

Rachel rolled her eyes. "You be good for your uncle Noah, okay?"

"Okay, Mommy. We're just gonna eat some food."

"Thanks, Noah. Please, no ketchup or mustard. I want him to look nice when we meet Sara Bennett."

"I'll do my best." He crouched down to Brad's level. "What'll it be, little dude? Burger and chips?"

"Yeah. Chips, too."

Rachel headed toward Adam and Cassie, who looked like they were having an intense conversation. As she got closer, their words carried clearly on the breeze.

"That's ridiculous." Adam rubbed the back of his neck. "I'm not staying on desk duty now that they've cleared me of all wrongdoing." He snapped a paper in his hand.

Cassie hooked her thumbs in her belt. "You'll follow the rules, Adam. Just like any other deputy in the department. I told you six months when I got home and heard about your shenanigans."

"Yeah? Well my *shenanigans* saved two kids, their grandmother and a crotchety aunt."

"Look, I'm glad the Texas Rangers, the FBI and Homeland Security are letting you off without any charges. You aren't even losing your badge. But you've still got three more months on desk duty."

He stormed off in the opposite direction without

another word. Rachel was tempted to chase after him, but Cassie waved her over.

"Hi, Rachel." Cassie lifted Daisy from her arms. "You're such a cutie, aren't you?" She tickled the baby's stomach.

"You heard back on Adam's situation, I take it."

"He makes me so furious sometimes. He's not losing his job. No charges are being filed against him. All the departments involved agreed that he didn't deserve to be punished for taking that hitman off the streets and turning in the cartel's money, regardless of how it was done. But he still wants to complain about *my* disciplinary decision of six months on desk duty. He's so doggone stubborn."

Rachel acted like she couldn't quite remember. "Why was he put on desk duty, originally?"

"He couldn't go out on the street until the decision came through." Cassie bounced Daisy on her arm, making the little girl giggle.

"And the decision was in his favor." Rachel tipped her head and squinted at Adam's sister. "So why another three months on the desk?"

"Because I told him six."

"Hmm." Rachel eased Daisy back onto her hip. "I guess stubbornness runs in the family." She smiled. "I've gotta go find Bree. The ceremony's going to start soon."

She left Cassie with her arms crossed, tapping a boot toe against the hot asphalt.

"Rachel!" Bree's voice called out over the crowd noise. "Over here."

Rachel turned toward the sound, then waved. She worked her way over to her friend, who stood next to a beautiful, sophisticated brunette in a lightweight summer suit.

Bree introduced them. “Rachel, this is Assistant District Attorney Sara Bennett.”

“Nice to meet you.” She shifted Daisy to her left arm and shook hands with the program’s benefactor.

“It’s a pleasure. And please, call me Sara.” She tickled Daisy’s chubby chin, and thankfully the child giggled instead of screamed.

“Rachel is head of our administrative department at the BCYP. She recently graduated with a degree in business, and I snapped her up before anyone else could hire her.” Bree beamed.

“That must have been quite the endeavor, along with taking care of a baby.” More tickles, more giggles.

Rachel blushed but didn’t reply. Apparently no need to, as Bree had her back.

“Oh, that’s nothing. She has a five-year-old son, too, and she worked full-time.”

“That *is* impressive. I had enough trouble with just college.” Sara laughed. “I’m so glad Bree brought you on board. You and Bree are the type of women who make programs like this successful. Dedicated, hardworking and intelligent. I can’t wait to get to know you better.”

A squeal from a microphone on the temporary stage pulled everyone’s eyes that way.

“Be ready next to the stage, okay, Rach? And stop acting so nervous. You already know almost everyone here. You'll do great." Bree ushered Sara toward the microphone.

"Ready for your moment in the spotlight?"

Rachel spun at the deep voice she loved.

Adam lifted Daisy from her arms and kissed his fiancée. "You look amazing."

"Eh, you're just saying that so I won't pawn my ring and run away to the glitter and glamour of big-city life." She held up her left hand, her ring reflecting the bright sunlight and blinding her for a moment.

"No regrets? You still have time to change your mind." He smoothed a wayward curl away from her cheek.

"Mm, let me think." She laid one finger against her chin and looked up at the sky, as if pondering the mysteries of the universe. "Nope. Sorry, you're stuck with me."

He held her gaze, his golden eyes declaring his love for her with no need for words.

"Hey, guys." Noah clapped a hand on each of their shoulders, breaking the intense moment. "One of you lose a contact or something?"

Rachel elbowed him in his side. "I guess I better get going. Bree won't be happy if I don't join them up there after our benefactor's speech."

Nate jostled Noah out of the way and stared up at the stage. "Hey, Rachel. Who's that stunning woman standing next to Bree? She looks kind of familiar."

"She's Cassie's friend, the attorney from Austin who contributed everything we needed to get the program rolling. Her name's Sara Bennett."

"No." Nate shook his head slowly. "No way. Sara Bennett?"

Noah eyed Nate. "Wasn't she Cassie's college roommate? The one she brought home on spring break one year? The one you—"

Nate grabbed Noah's arm and dragged him away before he could finish his sentence.

"What on earth was that all about?" Rachel asked Adam.

"Who cares? Get on up there, and let this town know how lucky it is to have three extraordinary women making a change for the better."

Rachel put her hand behind his neck, pulled him closer and gave him another quick kiss. "Don't tell anybody, but *I'm* the lucky one."

* * * * *